DEATH MATCH . . .

Knowing the man was quicker than he was, he did the only logical thing—something illogical. He threw his weapon straight at the samurai's grinning face. Instinctively, the man had to duck, blink, and block all at the same time. When his eyes opened, Casca had his sword wrist in one hand and his other arm around his back, twisting both. The samurai's arm came loose first at the shoulder as the sockets separated. Releasing his grip on the now useless and empty sword arm, Casca transferred his grip to the man's head. Grasping the samurai's topknot in his hand, he held the body rigid as he twisted, turning the man's head to an impossible angle. It gave way. The neck cracked . . .

The Casca series
by Barry Sadler

THE SAMURAI

BARRY SADLER

#19

JOVE BOOKS, NEW YORK

CASCA #19: THE SAMURAI

A Jove Book/published by arrangement with
the author

PRINTING HISTORY
Jove edition/April 1988

ISBN: 0-515-09516-8

Jove Books are published by The Berkley Publishing Group,
200 Madison Avenue, New York, New York 10016.
The name "JOVE" and the "J" logo
are trademarks belonging to Jove Publications, Inc.

PRINTED IN THE UNITED STATES OF AMERICA

10 9 8 7 6 5 4 3 2 1

CHAPTER ONE

The heavens broke open with the unchainable fury of the gods. To the east, thunderheads raced like black stallions draped in harnesses of lightning across seas swelling to the height of ten tall men on horseback. They rode the force called the Tai-fun. They had been sired deep in the wastes of the unknown seas where only barbarians and beasts dwelled. There they had gathered their strength and then sped across the vast gray waters, devastating all in their path, trampling all under their dark waves. Nothing was spared, for they had not the mortal weakness of mercy or the compassion for man, woman, child or animal. Alive or inanimate, all felt the power of their storm-driven hooves.

The cries of dying men had long since been silenced, swallowed up by the deep dark waters of the seas. Only bits of wrecked ships and the bloated bodies of men and horses wallowing in the swells gave any evidence that this place had once teemed with life. Those who had somehow made it to shore alive found no shelter from the winds that raged for three nights and then passed on across the waters to the land of the meat eaters and unclean ones.

The waters of Hakata Bay had long since been washed clean by the seas and by time when Jinto Muramasa stumbled over the black rocks seeking shelter for the night. His robes were of common-weave cotton fibers with the symbol of a mantis on the back. Dark stains and tears were evidence of recent battle. The Heiju Uprising against the Taira family had been crushed. All those who had supported the uprising were either dead or fleeing to await another day. He was one of those wandering mercenaries, a *ronin* who had cast his lot with the Minamoto clan and had lost, but then such is one's karma. The wheel of life would spin again and who knew what lots it would cast on the next turning. For now he needed a place to rest and something to eat. But shelter must come first. He knew these rocky shores from when he was a child and had played upon them more than once. There were many small caves set back from the waters in which one might rest and regain his strength. From the sea he would find the food he needed.

Spray whipped into a froth by the incoming tide washing ashore brought his eye to the sea and jagged coast. He squatted to look. Letting his eyes scan, forcing his body to relax, he opened his mind to the elements about him for a moment. It was empty; all was right. The birds flew as they should, diving and

swooping to feed upon small fish and then returning
to their nests in the rocks. Later he, too, would feed
on the small fish and the eggs of the birds. Wind
blew his hair, which hung loose. His *akagane* had
long since been lost during his flight. The cone-
shaped helmet of poor metal was no great loss except for the value it could have had to heat some
water to cook and wash in. *Aiie!* a hot bath. To be
massaged and rubbed, cleansed once more back into
a semblance of dignified humanity. He scratched at
fleas in disgust.

Scrambling crab-wise over a clump of boulders,
he found that which he sought. There in a crevice
where the waters at high tide were stopped was a
shadow. His shelter. Bending low, he climbed inside
the small cave. It was big enough for him to stretch
full out and still have room for two more men.
Squatting, he removed his robe, returned to the outside with it, and washed the poor cloth in saltwater.
Then he did his body. He stood, naked in the knee-
deep tide pool. He was short and dark with the
beginnings of a thin mustache. His arms were un-
usually muscled, proof of his heritage, of twenty-
five years at the forge, for his father had long ago
taught him the art of swordmaking and the ways of
steel. His face was angular, sharp corners etching
out prominent cheekbones and dark eyes slightly
bulbous with deep brown-black centers. The marks
of honorable wounds were in evidence, though none
were very deep. Along with the skill of making

swords, he had learned well the craft of using them, though he was not samurai. Perhaps one day? If the Minamoto had won, that is what he would have requested—the right to wear the *dai-sho*, two swords instead of his one good *jinto*, the war sword made by his father for him. Those who made the steel knew perhaps more than those of noble birth the true meaning of the *bushi*, the warrior's way and the mystic relation between a warrior and his blade.

Picking among the rocks, he caught several small scuttering crabs that he broke open and ate as he washed. The sweet flesh was still firm and vibrant. Raising his body, he returned to his cave. He placed his robe where it would catch the breeze and dry and then lay naked on his side, his *jinto* in his hand. He slept instantly.

It was three days before he felt his strength returning. The birds' eggs and the gifts of the sea had replenished his strength and the long sleep had given his body and spirit time to rest and heal. He avoided the few villagers he saw who came to fish on the coasts. It was not yet time to come out into the open. The warriors of Taira no Kiyomori, the *daidodaijin*, would not finish with the killing of those who supported the Minamoto for a long time to come. He thought for a time of stealing a boat to cross the waters to the land of the Chin where the Mongols ruled. But as with most of his race, he was not a good sailor, though he had made the journey once long ago with his father to buy iron of a special nature with which to make the prized *katana* blades for those of noble name. There they had spent over one year while his father visited with other sword smiths of the Kure, or as some called them, the Chin, and watched and learned. From this journey he had a bit of the tongue and could make some of his more basic wants known in the strange, lilting language.

Scavenging along the beach for what the morning tide might have brought in for him to eat, he saw a shape lying upon the dark sands. Covered with kelp, it was a form that he could not quite put a name to. There were bits of lighter color among the sour yellow-green of the giant seaweed. Moving closer, his hand close to his hilt, he stopped at a distance to watch. One never knew what lived in the depths of the sea. His trip to Chin had made him vow never to take the life of a seaman for his own. The thing twitched but made no other move. A wave came in soft and gentle, moving the kelp aside a bit.

Ah so deska! There was a hand under the kelp. And from the shape, now that he could see, it would appear also that there was a body to go with the hand. Perhaps this day would bring him good fortune. Perhaps the body would possess something of value to him. Almost anything would be of value now that he was in such dire straits.

He carefully checked the beach. No one. Moving over to the body, he removed the kelp, covering his nose from the odor. Beneath the soggy, greenish blanket was a man such as he had never seen before.

Almost like the Ainu of the northern islands, but different. The clothes were as those worn in Chin, a once simple and good robe of silk, but now rotted by salt and sun. His feet were bare and around his waist was a sword belt holding an empty sword sheath and a smaller one with a dagger in it. The body was disgusting. It was as bloated and pale as the belly of a sick fish. The flesh looked as if it would burst open if he pricked it with the point of his blade. And there were scars upon it. Many, many scars. The man had to have once been a powerful warrior to survive so many grievous wounds. But now that he had gone to whatever heaven or hell he believed in, he would have no further use for the small dagger. Twisting the body over to where he could better get at the grip, Muramasa saw the face. For a moment he thought he saw a muscle move in the mouth. But no. This one was long dead, probably three or four days.

It took both of his hands to roll the body over to where he could reach the handle of the dagger. Pulling the blade free from its sheath, he examined it with care and approval. He had not seen metal like this before, and the design was alien to him. He tested the point, careful not to draw blood, for there could be poison on it. And then he tested its flexibility. He was nearly able to bend the thin, pointed poniard in a quarter moon. The steel of Toledo was noted for its elasticity. He sucked in his breath in approval and started to put the dagger in the waistband of his *obi*.

Pain caused uncontrollable tears to come to his

eyes. It was so unexpected. Then fear. His hand was held in an ever-tightening grip by the corpse. Pale, dead flesh touched his and squeezed. Revulsion and terror raced through him. The thing on the beach was not man but an evil spirit and *iki-ryo*.

Forcing himself to look at the corpse, he saw the crusted lids open a fraction and pale eyes stare out at him. The mouth tried to force out words. There came only a thin, cracking sound. The grip on his wrist eased. The hand set him free and gently patted the back of his wrist as one would a well-loved child. It was not a threat, nor was there a threat in the eyes. Muramasa felt a great sadness in those strange-colored orbs. The dead man's hand dropped back to his side and the eyes closed.

Muramasa sat back on his heels, perplexed by this mystery. He could have simply taken his sword and hacked the man to pieces, but then the questions rolling around in his mind would never have an answer. His father had said long ago that he had been cursed with overweening curiosity. As he sat and pondered his dilemma, the man's body went into a spasm. The mouth opened and fluid poured forth, not only from the mouth but from the nose also. As it did, the scarred chest heaved and sucked in a great breath of air that sent shudders through it as though it had not breathed in a long time and had to learn the practice all over again. With the breath of air came a bit of color to the pale flesh as though once more the heart was pumping warm blood through long-still veins and arteries. Whatever this body was, it most assuredly was not dead any longer.

Muramasa sat beside the man for two hours, and with each minute the *gaijin*, the foreign one, seemed stronger. At last, unable to decide the issue, he contented himself to wait for the man, or whatever he was, to once more open his eyes and try to speak to him. He knew that the man would then be in need. Muramasa scrambled back along the beach into the rocks, returning to his cave. He brought back with him his water bottle, along with a few small crabs and a bit of fish caught the night before in a tidal pond. Settling back down, he resumed his vigil.

It was the time of the setting sun before the pale one opened his eyes again. His body moved with stiff limbs and the mouth opened dark as a demon's cave, his lips dry and cracked. Into that dark cave Muramasa poured a teacup amount of water, then waited and repeated the process several more times before the lips formed a strange word.

"Thank you."

He didn't understand the word but felt the meaning. He fed the man the fish and crabs in small pieces, one sliver at a time. The food seemed to work wonders on the pale one. In a matter of minutes, it was obvious that he was gaining his strength back. Soon he was sitting up and feeding himself, albeit with shaking fingers.

As much as he disliked touching the man, Muramasa forced himself to give him assistance in rising to his feet. Then he half led, half carried him back to the sanctuary of his cave in the rocks. Once there, the pale one again fell into deep sleep. Unsure of himself and why he had done what he had, Muramasa sat at the mouth of the cave with his sword. Bare legs crossed, he dozed knowing that any sound, even the smallest movement, would wake him instantly. He slept, comforted by the feel of his sword across his lap and the new knife of strange metal in his *obi*.

CHAPTER TWO

Forcing his eyelids open, the first sensation he had was of incredible pain. Sucking in his breath, he held it for a long time, slowly letting it out to fight the fire that burned like acid in every atom of his body. Through the haze of his pain, he could see a half-hunched shadow, a dark shape against the gray of a new day. He didn't remember who it was or even how he had gotten to where he was. All was a blur of half thoughts. One thing was certain: Someone had to have helped him.

By all the gods of every hell and heaven, he hurt. He fought back another wave of fire through his veins. What had happened? The last he knew he was hanging on to the hunk of timber after the ship of Chin went down. One minute it was fighting the storm, the next it was just gone, washed over by a monstrous wave. He had ridden out two days of the storm before things went blank. How long ago had that been? Now he was here, wherever here was. They had been going to the southern lands of the kingdom of Khmer when the winds blew them away from the shore and off course.

A groan forced its way between his clenched teeth.

Muramasa opened his eyes. *Ah so deska!*

Nodding his head politely to the pale man, he asked, "*Anata yoku nemutta ka?*"

Casca Longinus didn't have the faintest idea that he'd been asked if he'd slept well, but the tone was courteous. He bowed his head back. He'd spent enough years in the land of the Chin to know that basic courtesy and ritual between men.

Muramasa bowed his head again. "*Dai jobu*, very good." At least the barbarian had some iota of manners and it was good to have someone with him after his long time in hiding.

Sliding over to him, Muramasa handed him the water bottle and waited until the barbarian drank, noting the man, even though he was obviously in distress, did not drink all the water. He saved a fair portion and handed the bottle back, bowing his head again. "*Yoi*, very, very good." This might prove to be most interesting.

Casca noted the man's hand never left the hilt of his sword. Muramasa indicated a copper bowl by his side in which were pieces of raw fish cut into thin slivers and garnished with pieces of seaweed flavored with saltwater. It was all he had. Taking his time, Casca ate again, feeling the strength rush back into his limbs as the food was turned into energy.

Patiently, Muramasa sat in silence until the meager meal was finished.

Pointing at the bowl, the *ronin* said, "*Hashi.*"

Casca repeated the word and touched the bowl. "Very good, thank you." He bowed his head again.

Deciding to take a chance, though he didn't have to, Muramasa removed the poniard from his waistband, handing it over to Casca in the flat palm of his calloused hand.

Casca took the blade. It felt good to have a weapon with him once more. Noting the eyes of Muramasa, he hesitated only a moment before taking the blade and laying it in the palms of both open hands, offering it back to the smaller man and lowering his head and upper body as he did so. He knew the importance of such an offering in Chin where only one with complete confidence and trust would offer up his only weapon. And this man, though he wasn't exactly like those of the land of the Lotus, was similar enough that he thought they might have some of the same culture and habits in common.

For the first time, Muramasa released his grip on his sword and with both of his hands took back the Spanish dagger.

"*Ah domo arigato.*" He thanked Casca. He, too, knew what it meant for a fighting man, and this pale one was most certainly that, to give up his only weapon. It was an act of trust and confidence. Most proper under the circumstances.

Making signs, he indicated for Casca to rest while he went outside. It was time to scavenge for more food. Now that he had two mouths to feed, it would take a bit longer. Still it was promising to be a most interesting day. He would see if the barbarian could learn civilized speech. He seemed intelligent enough, and he would like to hear of distant lands and peoples. Ah, indeed. As his father had said, he was cursed with great curiosity. However, that too was his karma, and one could not fight what one was. Accept and enjoy.

It was three days before Casca left the small cave. During that time Muramasa taught him one word after another. By the time he was ready to go out, he basically understood that Muramasa was in hiding, having been on the losing side of a war. Well, that was a situation he was also familiar with. He had been hunted and enslaved more than once during his long, weary existence.

He helped Muramasa gather food, taking care to avoid being seen by the occasional peasant or fisherman who came to their section of the cove. As he did, the unnatural paleness of his skin quickly returned to normal as did his strength. He found nothing curious about Muramasa's eating habits. Raw fish and seaweed he'd ingested more than once. Food was food, though he wished now and then for a piece of rare beef. But it was not available, so he had to make do.

The days turned into two weeks, and by then they were able to make most of their wants known to each other. As always, Casca had a gift for tongues. He found the bandy-legged *ronin* a fascinating man. At times when Casca would be on watch, Muramasa would go through training exercises with the sword that he called a *katana*. It was hard to recall when or even if he'd seen better or more interesting sword play. Everything was a ritual, but a most deadly one he had no doubt. Muramasa had his share of scars to prove it. Casca knew that it would take many years of training to handle a sword the way Muramasa did. It was not something to be learned with ease. It was an art. Still he felt his own techniques would serve him well enough if push came to shove. They always had in the past. It was during one of these exercises when Casca saw a gleam reflect from behind an outcropping of black boulders a hundred meters away. Then another.

He was too far away to warn Muramasa without letting those who were sneaking up on him among the rocks know that they had been seen. Sliding down between a pair of black boulders covered with small grayish lichens, he began working his way away from the beach. Moving at an angle, which he hoped would put him to the intruders' rear and flank, he speculated on how many there were. This might be an opportunity to get himself refitted with clothes and weapons that he desperately needed. It was damned uncomfortable crawling around on the rocks with only a loincloth for a cover.

Standing between the boulders where the surf just lightly touched his feet, Muramasa seemed oblivious to all except his sword rituals. The square angles of his face were forced into stern lines; the corners of his mouth went down in a ferocious scowl as though he were very angry and on the verge of exploding inside. The *katana* shimmered in the early light as he sliced through bodies that weren't there. Attack, counter, slice, withdraw, and attack again.

Keeping as low as he could, Casca raised his head. There they were! Now he could see all of them. There were three men who looked very much like Muramasa, except their robes were in good condition and gray in color with an ideogram on the breasts and backs he couldn't recognize. One had a strange-looking helmet on, almost like the shell of a turtle secured on his head by a bright blue cloth tied beneath his chin. The other two were obviously lesser types as they followed the turtle helmet's every hand signal instantly. Their heads were bare, the hair having been partially shaved away leaving a peculiar-looking scalp lock. All of them had two blades with them—a long sword much like Muramasa's in their hands, and smaller ones of the same slender, slightly curving shape, about the length of a Roman gladius, stuck in the waistbands of their robes.

He would have liked to have warned Muramasa, but to do so would have given his position away. With three of them, surprise was needed. If he could time it right, he'd still be able to give Muramasa warning before they attacked.

Sliding his body over the cold, wet boulders, he slid like a snake. It wasn't too difficult. The three men's attention was on Muramasa, who continued with his exercises. When they reached the last line of boulders, separating them from the beach where Muramasa worked his sword play, they hesitated a moment, conferring with hushed voices and gestures. Casca knew that turtle head was giving them their instructions. He was about fifteen feet behind them, gathering his legs under him, ready to make a lunge and take out at least one of them, then get his weapon and give Muramasa time to come to his aid. He was still preparing to lunge when without warning they burst out at a run. Swords held high, they raced at Muramasa, who seemed oblivious to all about him. Casca started to yell a warning when Muramasa turned faster than anything he'd ever seen, making his movement still seem no more than a part of his exercises. He whirled down and came up with a two-handed stroke Casca had never seen before. It sliced an attacker's sword arm off. Coming up from under the armpit without ceasing his movement, he circled back around, ready for the others. The man who had just lost his arm stood still for a moment, gazing with wonder at his limb lying on the black sand, the hand still holding the grip of his *katana*. Then he fell to his knees and waited to die as his life's blood poured from the amputated shoulder.

The other two were on Muramasa, not hesitating for their wounded comrade. They tried to get Muramasa between them. His sword flickered around them, parrying, thrusting, slicing, blocking every strike they made. Casca was on his feet, moving. With their concentration on Muramasa, they didn't hear the hiss of his feet on the sand. He grabbed the upraised sword arm of the one with the scalp lock. Twisting him around, he struck him across the throat with his left elbow, crushing the larynx. Ripping the sword from his hand, he turned to aid Muramasa.

The turtle head was just now aware the game had changed. Backing off, he lowered his *katana* to where its tip nearly touched the earth and sucked in a great breath of air, preparing himself to meet both of them. There was no fear in his eyes beneath the comical helmet. Only deadly acceptance of his karma.

With a shake of his head, Muramasa told Casca to stay out of it. Setting forward, his body at right angles, he raised his *katana* in a two-handed grip, stepping forward with a sliding dance motion. The turtle head countered. They began to move slowly, gracefully.

Casca knew that Muramasa was treating him to an object lesson in the art of the sword. He squatted down, sitting on the back of the man he'd just killed to watch the two men on the beach engage in their dance of death. He had to admit it was beautiful. Never had he seen such style. They would instantly rush, meet, their swords ringing off each other, then be on opposite sides again, sucking in air, growling beneath their breath as they gathered themselves again. Then once more they rushed at each other, both with upraised blades held in double hands, and it was over.

Casca wasn't sure he'd seen the stroke. One second Muramasa's sword was in the air above his head. Then he was down in a whirling motion and coming back up, the razor edge slicing open the turtle head from groin to chest. And then he was back in his preparatory stance with upraised blade, his face calm, expressionless, except for a glazed look to the eyes as if he'd just reached the peak of sexual satisfaction.

Turtle head dropped to his knees, his sword falling from his hands as he tried to hold bulging intestines from spilling out of his abdomen. He raised his eyes to Muramasa and spoke a few words rapidly. Muramasa grunted and bowed his head slightly. Stepping forward to the man's side, he waited. Turtle head half bowed from the waist, extending his head out, baring the nape of the neck. Instantly the *katana* in Muramasa's hand flashed again. The head fell free, the mouth open and moving as if it had one last thing it wanted to say. Then the body slumped forward.

Reaching into his robe top, Muramasa removed a silk cloth and carefully wiped the blood from his sword. Then with a quick, sure movement, he reversed the blade and slid it into its scabbard, signifying everything was finished.

CHAPTER THREE

Muramasa moved to his kills. After separating the head of the man with one arm, he began stripping the bodies. Nodding his head at Casca, he indicated for him to do the same to the man he'd killed. Casca went to it with alacrity, glad to don the robes of the dead samurai. They were a bit small, but as they wore them loose here, they'd fit well enough.

Best of all were the weapons: a long sword, a *katana* similar to Muramasa's, and a shorter one Muramasa called a *tachi*. Inside the robe was a small red silk purse with several silver coins and a few of copper. He had money again. Just the touch of it made him feel more like a civilized man of means.

When they finished stripping the bodies of all of value, Muramasa glanced at the sea. The tide was beginning to go out. With Casca's help, he moved the bodies into the water, letting the ocean take them out from where, with luck, they would never return. The heads being heavier than water, Muramasa simply tossed them out as far as he could, leaving it to the crabs to clean them up.

Gathering their spoils, they returned to their cave to figure out what their next course of action would be.

By words, signs, and grunts, Muramasa made it clear they had to move. The long arm of someone or something called Taira had reached out for him. Casca thought it most likely they had been spotted by a peasant who turned them in for a reward. But then it could have just been an accident the three samurai had come along when they did. But it was best not to count on accidents. Making up two packs of their goods, they left the cave, Muramasa taking him along a narrow black-rock path away from the ocean and island. Once they were in the open, Muramasa moved with strong, long, sure strides for someone who was a bit bow-legged, and Casca had to struggle to keep up with him. His strength had not fully returned. He stuck his two new swords in his waistband as he saw Muramasa do. He didn't know that to any samurai who saw them wearing their swords in such a fashion it was a deadly insult, which could only be answered with death. But he was now a *ronin* too, though he still didn't understand just what it meant to be a *ronin*. They were outside the law and most would die while still quite young, unless they found a master to attach themselves to.

The wearing of the two swords meant nothing to

Casca. He'd done it before a dozen times; a long blade and a short one were normal, but to Muramasa it was something that ate at his soul. True, he wore the *bushi*, but he was not entitled to them. He would, if he lived long enough, one day be *samurai*. That he swore to himself long ago. He would have the right to wear the two swords before he died, and to be ready for that time he had to have a plan. Perhaps the pale scar-faced one would be of help in this matter. For to be noticed by the great men, the *daimyos*, one had to be special. With the pale strange-looking barbarian beside him, he would most certainly be noticed no matter where he went. That, of course, could also prove to present some problems, as it would not be long before the samurai and hirelings of the Taira family knew of his exisitence. But then again, as always, it was what was in one's karma that really mattered; nothing could change that.

Leading the way, skirting the scattered villages, Muramasa took him away from the coast, climbing higher into the range of blue-hazed mountains lying a few miles inland. From what he saw, the countryside was similar to the lands of Chin—square, carefully tended fields of rice and small plots of vegetables. In most fields men and women in baggy clothes worked bent over, moving in a rythym as old as the land they worked.

When anyone approached them, Muramasa would move off the rails away from them before they could get close enough to get a good look at his strange companion. It was not yet time to let the world know of him. That must be delayed yet a time longer, then it would not matter.

They traveled all that day and into the night, making camp by a waterfall that cascaded down in bright sparkles of light, laying a fine mist over them.

A small fire hidden from view by a ring of boulders helped to drive away some of the chill. Casca was more than pleased that he'd been fortunate enough to acquire some new clothes. If they had to come up here dressed as he had been, it would have been a most uncomfortable night. As it was, it was a hungry night, but Muramasa didn't make any protest and neither did he, though he did look at the pond by the waterfall, wondering if there might be fish in it. Deciding to try his luck in the morning, he cut a branch from a tree and with his shorter blade whittled out a fish spear using pieces of split bamboo to make a pronged trident.

Muramasa wrapped his extra robe about him, ignoring Casca. The robe was his. He felt no need to offer any part of it. Placing his *katana* close to his body, hand on the hilt, he closed his eyes, taking in a deep breath, then letting it out slowly to clear his mind and open it for the night's sleep.

Casca did the same. Resting his back against a moss-covered boulder, he rested his head on his knees, his own sword close to hand, and wondered what the next days would bring. There was something about these new people that was much different than the Chin. They were quicker, more dynamic, and they killed without hesitation. He would have to learn all he could if he was to avoid a duel every time he turned around.

Before dawn his eyes opened along with his ears. The rustle of brush brought him up and around, sword in hand. Muramasa was coming back from the pond, Casca's fish spear in one hand and a string of fat fish strung through the gills on a green reed in the other.

Casca felt a bit put out that he had not awakened when Muramasa left the camp and even more because he had not had a chance to use the spear that he'd made. But after a breakfast of fresh fish wrapped in mud and baked in the coals of their morning fire, he felt in a forgiving mood.

By signs and gestures, Muramasa made it known that they were going high into the mountains to a place he'd been before with his father who had been a swordsmith. The father was dead now and that was all Casca got out of him.

After they crossed the first range of mountains, Muramasa left him for a time to go into a village where he bought food. He brought back rice beans and a white jelly-looking stuff which to Casca had no taste at all, but Muramasa smacked his lips in relish over the bean curd cakes he called *tofu*.

They saw no one after three more days of travel, but they did pass a few small stone shrines on the way where offerings of flowers had been made, showing that this trail was used from time to time by others. Toward evening of the second day, Muramasa pointed to a small valley set between green vibrant hills. Following his finger, Casca saw a hut and a small plot of land that looked overgrown and untended. It was clear from the flush on Muramasa's face that they were nearing their destination.

Striding forcefully forward, Muramasa went to the thatch-roofed house and swung open the sliding doors which were panels of rice paper, long since eaten away, leaving only thin dirty rags hanging from weathered frames. Removing his *tabi*, he entered the house with bare feet, bowing his head in honor of the memory of his father.

All was bare, long since it had been stripped of its few possessions and furniture by passersby. That did not bother Muramasa, for it was the memory that mattered, not the physical things of his life here in the mountains above the sea.

Leaving the house, he went to the rear of the hut. There was what he had hoped he would find buried beneath an anvil of ancient stone. His father's tools: his hammer and the round steel rod for polishing the *mikagi-hari*. But most important was what they had brought back from the land of Chin so many years ago—the foreign metal. It would be the heart of the sword, the core metal, the *shintetsu*. There was enough for one more sword, a master blade into which he would pour his soul, forging his spirit into the red-hot steel. He would make a blade equal to the grass-cutting sword of Prince Yamato-dake, the Kusunagi no Tsurugi of ancient legend.

Motioning the *gaijin* forward, he began to explain that here they would work and the pale one would assist him. It took a bit of doing, but at last Casca understood. Muramasa was going to do something special.

As if to say the condition of the house did not matter, Muramasa had them make camp outside near the forge. He would permit them this one last day to rest, for on the morrow they would begin.

With dawn, Muramasa began to gather what he would require. There were small piles of the special pine charcoal left from time past. The small bellows of skin had to be repaired from where the rats had eaten at it. And the entire area had to be purified to drive away any spirit who might try to interfere with his work or cause him evil. Curious, Casca stood aside during most of this, watching Muramasa move from one place to another, bowing, going to his knees and chanting. There was a great deal of gesturing and arm-waving involved. Casca knew what was going down and knew it was best if he just stayed out of the way until Muramasa needed him. This was between the *ronin* and his gods and not something for an outsider.

At last Muramasa seemed to be satisfied. From nooks and crannies he scurried until he had what he needed to begin. First he made a *hina-gata*, a template of wood, a model to guide his thoughts as he worked the metal. The *hina-gata* would hang where it was always in his sight and mind. Then would come the preparation of the fire. Every move was a ritual that had been prescribed and truly followed for hundreds of years. There was no variance permitted. A thing was either right or it was not. There was no middle ground or mistakes.

Casca would be the first *gaijin* to ever witness the making of a *katana*. It would be long centuries before another was so honored.

CHAPTER FOUR

It was almost time. All was in readiness for the work to come. Muramasa deemed it exceedingly good fortune and a blessing when his father's long-time servant and assistant at the forges showed his stooped body at their campfire the night before he was to begin work on his *katana*. Gray was the color of him to Casca's eyes. Everything about the old man was gray. His clothes, hair, and skin, the color of ashes long dead.

Hama-san barely controlled his pleasure at seeing the son of his master. It was with difficulty that he fought back tears. Ever since Muramasa's father had died, he had come to this lonely place on holy days to place his small offerings of rice by the springs where the ashes of his master lay in rest. This was to placate and show reverence for the *kami* of the springs whose water had tempered his blades for over forty years. It was here his memories of happiness were the strongest, when he and Muramasa's father had worked the red-white steel, side by side.

The old smith gave only one long inquiring look

at Casca, to which Muramasa responded in quick, short bursts. Hama-san bobbed his head in agreement with whatever Muramasa had said, and that was the end of the matter. He placed his woven straw mat down by the fire, spread a weathered and patched *futomi* over him, and went to sleep. There would be much work in the morning. Hama-san, who had worked at the side of Muramasa's father for over forty years, was in attendance. His wrinkled, leathery face was a map of his life and times. The eyes were barely visible as black chips of obsidian peering through folds of skin that had been baked over the coals of the fire since he had been a child.

Casca stood by, not knowing exactly what it was he was expected to do, but he had no doubt that Muramasa would let him know when the time came.

Under Muramasa's instructions, all had been purified, including those who would work the steel. They wore their best clothes, such as they were. Hands were scrupulously cleaned, even to the paring of the fingernails, so that no impurity would contaminate the event which was about to take place. Hama-san nodded to Muramasa. The color of the coals was right. It was time to begin.

The first block of iron was put into the coals to slowly gain life, changing colors under the ever-constant watch of the two smiths. Their faces changed with the metal as the glow of the coals cast wavering shades of red over them. Hama-san did not have to be told when the metal was right. Taking the glowing block of metal between the lips of well-used copper tongs, he set it upon a small anvil, holding it firm as Muramasa drew in a deep hissing breath. He raised his hammer and made the first of ten thousand blows which would, if the gods were pleased, change a lifeless piece of metal into a living thing of beauty and death.

Casca became trapped in a seemingly never-ending cycle of fire, coals, and the smell of hot metal being molded and formed. At times which only he selected, for reasons unknown to Casca, Muramasa would add a piece of the foreign steel to the mass, then hammer the block, each process lengthening the steel, stretching it out, then once more bending it back on itself, welding it to its own soul. Again and again the process was repeated with frequent bathings in purest spring water from his father's well. Each of the smiths took turns tasting and smelling the spring water repeatedly, making many signs and grunts before they proclaimed it suitable for their labors. Casca lost himself in the process as the two men worked day after day, permitting him at times to hold the tongs as Hama-san aided Muramasa in the forming of the steel, which after six days began to take on a shape unto itself.

Two weeks passed as the three men worked over the small forge, and each day the blade became more than it was the previous day. They were trapped in a web of fire and hammering. Casca tried to keep track of the times Muramasa had bent and fused the white-hot metal back on itself, then stretched it out again. He had repeated the process over and over.

The number of fusions that were building up in ever-thinner layers was too great for him to count. Never had he seen a blade made in this fashion.

At last, during the hour before dawn, Muramasa left the forge. In his hand was the blade, still to be polished and sharpened, but it was without a doubt a thing of beauty. Holding the naked *tang* in his hand, Muramasa could feel the life still waiting to be born within it. It was his first. It was his child. It was a Muramasa blade!

The polishing and sharpening of the blade took three days, during which time Hama-san worked on the fittings. He would have preferred to use a bit of gold to make the mountings, but there was none to be had. He did use several of the silver coins they had taken from the samurai they had killed on the beach. Muramasa was careful to ask Casca if it was all right to use the coins, for part of them were his by right of his kill. Casca agreed. He would do nothing to interfere with what the two forge-burned smiths were doing. He had to see the ending.

With the silver coins, Hama-san made *shibuichi*, a mixture of brass and silver to form the *tsuka,* the guard, in which he inlayed a willow tree over a tiny spring. It was graceful and delicate to honor the waters which had given the sword its strength. The hilt was of two carefully selected, matched pieces of wood with identical grain from the *ho-no-ki* tree and covered with a single section of pale, ghost-colored *sami*, the bubbled skin of the ray fish.

When all was ready, Hama-san and Muramasa

began to assemble the blade into its final form, the *habaki*, blade socket, *seppa*, washers of copper, then the *tsuka*. The last to be applied were the wrappings, *uichi-himo*, strong blue silk braid a quarter of an inch in width. All was ready. The *fuchi*, or collar, and the *kashira,* or pommel cap, were in place. The pins were set. The *katana* was finished.

Muramasa held it in his hands taking the primary stance. Both hands set firm on the long hilt, he drew in his breath and began to move through the proscribed ritual cuts permitted a samurai. The weapon was good, better than any he had ever felt. But it was as a child in the womb waiting to be born. There was life in the steel, but it was not yet alive. Something was missing or needed to be done. He didn't know just what, but the blade was unfinished. There was something more. Why he thought the *katana* needed more than he had done he couldn't tell. But in the forming of the weapon he could sense that it was going to be something different, special in some manner. Disappointed, he sat on his haunches and looked at the *gaijin*, shaking his head slowly, side to side.

"I do not know," he repeated over and over. Casca didn't know what he was talking about. To him the *katana* was a work of incredible art and beauty. What could possibly be wrong with it?

There was little sleep that night, though the three should have gone deeply into the comfort of Morpheus. All were restless with an uneasy feeling of something left undone. At last Muramasa rose while the night was still on them and first light a half hour yet in the distant future.

Catching Casca's wakeful eye, he walked to the edge of the trees surrounding their camp. Taking the katana with him, Muramasa motioned for Casca to join him. Together they walked through the dark hills between graceful, sweeping pines. The night was clean. But the new day when Ameratsu cast her first light was incredible. Mist rose from the soft spongy earth, fronds and leaves bent heavy with night dew. The rich smell of good earth rose to meet the new day. The first day since the sword was completed. Still Muramasa wore a troubled expression. There was something between him and the sword that could not be put into words. Something left undone.

He led the way through a green crystal glen. Halting at the edge of the glen, he touched Casca lightly on the forearm with his fingertip. It was a soft, gentle gesture. Then by sign and word, he let Casca know that this was where the spring was. His well. It had belonged to his father and his father before him. Near the spring Casca saw two small simple carved-stone pillars about a meter high resting on squared bases of stone. He knew this was where the ashes of Muramasa's father were layed to rest.

Muramasa felt a swelling in his throat and chest as he looked at the well. It was from here they had always drawn the water to temper their blades. It was not to be drunk from. That would be to defile it. This was a sacred place and human lips were unclean. Muramasa pointed to the other side toward a cleft in the rocks where a small shrine was garnished with fresh flowers from offerings he and Hama-san had made during the forging process. They were made to honor and placate the *kami* who lived in the well during the purification rituals of the spring water.

Casca could feel the peace of the glen. Birds sang softly in the tree branches, cool, green ferns flourished with abandon among small scarlet flowers with dark eyes on their petals. There was a feel to this place that was different, special. He had felt such things only a few times in his life. Perhaps Muramasa was right and a spirit did live in this quiet place of delicate sounds and lush greenery, listening eternally to the soft music of the bubbling natural well.

Grasping Casca's arm, he hissed for silence and drew him back into the shadows of the pines. Casca could feel Muramasa's body tense. Then he saw what it was that had caused him to draw back to where they were unseen.

Two men in tattered robes furtively edged out of the other side of the glade. One had a bared sword, the other a long-bladed halbard type of spear over his shoulder. Casca knew it was called a *naginata*. He also had a shorter kind of blade about a foot long stuck into his waistband, what Muramasa had called an *obi*. Casca knew trash when he saw it. It mattered not what country he was in. These two were scum. He could almost smell their unwashed bodies as they cautiously entered the glade. Besides their obvious weapons, each had a bundle tied over his shoulder that contained, Casca guessed, all their worldly possessions, which was probably more than he had.

Keeping one eye on the men and the other on Muramasa, he thought he saw the beginning of a tremble in Muramasa's sword hand. Odd, he'd never seen any overt expression of anxiety before in the mostly silent man—not even when they'd killed the samurai by the sea. Then he'd acted as if it had been of no more importance than having a normal breakfast, nothing at all to be excited about.

Muramasa felt the tremor in his hand also, but it didn't seem to be coming from him. Yet there was a definite movement, as with something coming awake. The feeling was almost as that of lightning. Once, when he was a child of eight years, a bolt from the gods had struck close to him, blasting a tree into cinders and ashes, leaving his body tingling, numb, and aching. It was almost that kind of sensation that trickled up his arm into his chest, making his heart beat a bit faster.

The two men worked their way cautiously closer to the well. They moved much like animals of a lower order, partially bent over, eyes jerking back and forth in their skulls. As they moved closer to the spring, Muramasa felt his pulse beat quicken in his temple, his face began to grow hot and flushed, and the tremor increased in his hand. He could not control the feelings coming over him. Never had he been so weak as not to be able to control a shake in his hand or leg. What he felt inside was an increasing rage. His hand tightened on the handle of his sword and the blade trembled heavily in response.

The smaller of the two men, the one with the sword, was at the edge of the well. His comrade stood behind him facing the way they had come. Perhaps they were being pursued? The smaller man gave his head a quick furtive jerk from side to side as he took one last look around. Then he knelt on all fours to drink from the well as a dog would, lapping the crystal water into loose lips, sucking in the cool clean fluid between slime-whitened gums.

Coming to his feet, Muramasa recognized the feeling coming over him. It was rage—white-hot rage that filled his soul. Not thinking, he began to run forward, sword in hand, the new steel flashing clean in the bright air. He moved as never before. How dare those unclean things drink from the well of his father. On silent feet he was on the man before Casca was able to rise fully to his feet and follow. The smaller man sensed something. He began to rise from all fours, his right hand starting to raise his sword. He was half erect when Muramasa reached him. The trembling in his hand had now reached all of his body. Within and without, he was shaking with fury, with a need to cleanse the filth before him from the face of the sacred land. His sword rose. He didn't control it. It was not his thinking that guided the weapon. His body followed the movement of the blade. Then it swung down as his breath was exhaled between clenched teeth.

The cut was from the junction of the neck just

above the seventh vertebra, then through the collar-
bone, angling to the sternum, slicing through the
cartilage and spinal column, then beneath the float-
ing rib the blade came forth. The smaller man slid in
two pieces to the green earth. The motion was not
stopped when the sword cut through the drinking
man. It continued of its own volition, coming back
in an up-hand angle strike that took the gaping man's
arm off at the shoulder, then continuing in a smooth
sweep. The blade turned in midair as Muramasa
followed it. The steel sliced through the man's neck.
The movement was so rapid that the man's arm had
not yet reached the earth when the blade was already
in his neck, separating it from his shoulders to fall
dully to the grass beside his arm. The severed neck
spouted a scarlet-foaming fountain from the open
arteries, as the mouth jerked open and closed with
the blinking of the man's eyes. It would be a few
seconds before the head knew it was dead.

The enemy was dead, but Muramasa could not
control the passion within him. It kept his arms
rising and falling. The steel of the *katana* dipped
deep, slicing and tearing away at the already dead
flesh at his feet. Then as it had come, it was gone,
slowly draining away from his face, shoulders and
arms. Leaving him, this time, trembling naturally.

He turned to face his barbarian companion, his
robes splattered with blood. Casca paid no attention
to the mangled corpses at the edge of the well. It
was Muramasa's face that captured him. The expression was beatific, sexual, as if he had achieved the

ultimate sensual experience. He didn't understand, but Hama-san, who had come upon the scene seconds before Muramasa attacked the interlopers, knew what had occurred.

There had been something left undone. The pure water of the well was not enough for this blade. It demanded blood. It had a karma of its own. It would have to drink and drink forever as long as a hand would carry it. Hama-san shivered at the thought.

Muramasa raised the bloody *katana* above his head. Thick red gore ran down the shining steel to collect in clots on the sleeves of his *hakata*.

Voice hoarse, rasping, he cried out in pride and anguish as Ameratsu hid behind a cloud, as if she did not wish her sacred light to witness what defilement had occurred on the spring.

"Now you are truly tempered and you have chosen your name. *WELL DRINKER!*"

CHAPTER FIVE

From the west, winds blew through the needles of the pine trees, bringing with them the promise of rain. For now it was only pleasantly cool, but with the night a heavier chill might come.

Muramasa squatted by the charcoal brazier, his face empty, void of all emotion. He was resting from his labors, for the work had been long and hard. He had poured his soul into the making of the blade, which lay before him on a clean white cloth of cotton. By the flickering light of the charcoals, it wavered and moved. The steel was alive as nothing he had ever experienced was alive. It had a soul. He knew it. He could feel it. This was not a normal blade, for it had been born in blood. *Aiie*, he was almost afraid of it, but as with many things one feared, he was irresistibly drawn to it.

Across the fire, the face of the barbarian was red and glowing. It was an incredibly ugly face with the gray eyes and the scar running down the side of it. And the hair was washed out and was pale and unhealthy looking. In spite of all that, he felt somehow it was a good face. And for a barbarian, he had the good manners to say nothing at this delicate moment.

At last, deep bone-draining weariness settled over him. Making an effort to keep the words simple, he told Casca that it was time to sleep for their work was done here. On the morrow they would travel far to the north. Grunting his understanding, Casca lay back under their shelter, wrapping his thin robes about him, and waited for the sleep to come. He knew that Muramasa wanted some time alone with his thoughts. It was well enough. He was tired, and with the refreshing winds and rain to come, he knew he would sleep well this night and be ready for what the next day might bring.

The rains did come but they were gentle, restful, as the drops fell in easy patterns from the tips of pine needles to scent the earth and the air. He had learned much during the time of the sword making. A word, a phrase here and there. Not perfect, but they were beginning to understand more about each other, though to tell the truth, Casca found Muramasa to be as much of a mystery and as fascinating as any man he'd ever met. Never had he seen such concentration as he and his old helper had on their faces when they worked the steel. He also saw the first sign of fear on one of their faces when, after returning from the spring, the helper had, with Muramasa's permission, touched the blade now called *Well Drinker*. Instantly, as if the blade were fresh from the coals, he jerked back his weathered hand, looked at Muramasa, bowed his head, gathered his few belongings, and left the camp without another word, not even looking back. Casca wondered what had gone on but couldn't fathom it.

Overhead the clouds moved in, luminescent at first, then growing darker. The back of his mind was aware for some time that Muramasa did not sleep, that he walked the night with the new sword of his making in his hands. Sometimes he thought he heard voices and could only speculate that Muramasa was talking to the gods or his father's spirit as he knew was the custom among the Chin.

Muramasa did indeed speak to the gods and his father that night. He railed at them and prayed for guidance. He threatened to cast the sword into a lake but knew he could not. And as always, he found at last that he could not escape his karma. What was to be, would be. The sword was with him and they would gather their few belongings together and leave the camp. When first light came, Muramasa did not look back either. It was as if he were leaving something behind and had no wish to return. A part of his life was finished and something new was to come. He was not the same man as he had been the day before. Something awaited him.

When Casca asked Muramasa where they were going, Muramasa only growled in his fashion and pointed to the north. "Yoritomo Minamoto." That was it, and Casca guessed it had to be enough. He hitched his pack a bit higher on his shoulder. It was a little heavier now. The additional weapons they had acquired from the dead men by the spring and their few belongings gave them sufficient provisions to make their way for some time.

As Casca had guessed, they were outlaws of some kind. They had with them several different coins of value including three small pieces of gold. If they had to they could sell the dead bandits' swords, to eat, even though they were of poor quality and not nearly the temper of the swords they'd taken by the sea.

Their first day's march they kept to the mountain trails, though often they could see the sparkling blue of the sea in the distance. Muramasa led the way with long, certain strides. He moved as a man with a mission. Casca just brought up drag, not really having any other choice. Whatever Muramasa was going to do he was involved in it. That was enough for now.

Twice in three days Muramasa traded off some of their captured goods for food and better clothing. He seemed to have suddenly decided that they needed a more prosperous appearance. The poorly made blades of common iron were not worth robes of silk but they did bring each of them two outfits of good-quality cotton, though Casca would have preferred a combination other than trousers of deep plum set off by a yellow and black striped tunic. Muramasa took the better grade of clothes for himself, which he deemed as only his right, for he was without a doubt the leader of their two-man expedition. And it was painfully obvious that his companion was at best a

higher grade of low-class barbarian and should therefore be satisfied with anything he was given.

On midday of the fourth day, Muramasa became a
bit uneasy as they came down from the mountains.
He pointed to a valley below where neat squared
paddies were filled with young green rice sprouting
as far as the eye could see until the fields reached the
more brackish lands of the beach. Squatting on his
haunches, Muramasa screwed his face up tight in
deep concentration. Looking first back over his shoulders to the mountain path, then back down to the
valley, Casca thought he was trying to make up his
mind which was the best route to take. The nights
were cold in the mountains, though neither complained. What concerned Muramasa was that the
going was becoming slower. At last Muramasa arose,
shook his broad shoulders, and pointed down to the
valley. With a grunt he spoke one word, "Taira,"
and touched the handle of his sword, *Well Drinker*.
Casca understood him. Whoever was master down
there was the ally of the Taira, whose clan Muramasa
had been fighting against and had been hunted by.

Whatever Muramasa had in mind, he was in a
hurry, and to journey the mountain trails was eating
up too much time. They would take the valley road
and hope for the best.

As for Casca, his eyes were full of everything
new. He'd not seen very much of this strange land of
small, intense people, only a few villages from the
distance which did not appear to be very much different from those he'd seen in the southern parts of

Chin. Though he had the feeling that if all the men of this strange land were as intense as Muramasa, they would be very hard to deal with if they ever got together on a single project.

Two hours before sunset they had reached a good well-traveled road. Casca drew many curious stares from the peasants they passed, but none stopped or questioned them. For the two strangers carried swords. They would leave any questions to others with swords. And as Casca's luck would have it, that's exactly that they ran into. Coming their way were three men on horseback wearing armor of a kind he'd never seen before: over-lapping plates of red and black trimmed with gold, broad helmets of the same colors and face guards that gave them the aspect of demons. The leader was obviously more richly dressed than the two warriors escorting him. Over his armor was a surcoat of rich light-blue silk and over that a longer robe of brilliant rainbow colors interwoven into a hunting scene with many swans, cranes, and waterfowl. His face, like the others, was covered by a mask that showed only his obsidian eyes peering fiercely through the slits.

When they spotted Muramasa and Casca, they reined up their horses, blocking the road.

Casca had been in too many of these situations not to recognize trouble when he saw it. Just the angles of their bodies and their postures meant these men were not going to let them go easily. He shifted his pack so it would be easier to drop and adjusted the grip on the *naginata*. It would be of more use against mounted horsemen than his sword. The leader of the horsemen called out to them. He couldn't recognize the words but the tone of contempt and anger was clear.

Muramasa stood his ground, his back tensing. Under his robes he flexed his muscles, loosening them up while on the surface he appeared calm and detached as Sakai Taira spoke to him as if he were no more than the dust under his lowest samurai's feet.

"Ho, dog. These are my lands and I have given no one permission to use my roads or carry weapons on them."

Muramasa bowed slightly, only a half bow, a deliberate insult.

"I regret that we found no one to ask permission of. But as you see, we are only poor wandering men of no value. We seek no problems and apologize most deeply if we have offended any by our presence." The words were mild but Sakai knew they were not sincere. He was being mocked by this unclean thing before him. However, the *ronin* and his incredibly ugly and large barbarian companion might provide him and his samurai a few moments of diversion.

"It matters not who you might have asked. For I have already judged and condemned you. For I am Sakai Taira, kinsman, guardian, and lord of this province for Taira seii-Taishogun. *Wakarimasu ka*?"

Muramasa bobbed his head up and down. "*Hai, so desu*?" As he acknowledged that he did understand, he dared to question whether all that Sakai had said was indeed a fact.

Sakai could not tolerate such disrespect from this *eta*, this handler of dead things and offal. He was beneath his attention. To his *goke'nin*, he would give the opportunity to cleanse his road for him. As his sworn vassals they had only one duty, and that was to do his bidding at the cost of their lives if he so wished. To fail to do his bidding was to achieve the same end, only in an extremely more unpleasant manner.

He spoke, barely able to control the anger in his body. "Kill those things which walk like men, but smell as if they are already long dead."

Without pause the two horsemen instantly spurred their mounts on, drawing their swords at the same time they rushed down on Muramasa and Casca. Dropping his pack, Casca moved to the side of the road, jumping on a small ridge, a channel used to irrigate the rice fields, giving him a couple of more feet in height and forcing the on-rushing riders to come to him on his ground. They would have to rein up or their horses would go over the side into the rice paddies.

He needn't have worried too much about both of them reaching him. As they rode down on them, Muramasa drew *Well Drinker*, made a low, whirling movement with his body, dropped to knee level in a powerful swing, then twisted his body up, leaping into the air at the exact time the lead rider reached him. The lead samurai's sword was on the downswing when *Well Drinker* came into contact with his body at the waist. The impetus of the horse gave the razor-edged *katana* all the force it needed to slice through the plates of lacquered armor as if they were thin silk. It entered the softer, warmer tissue beneath with enough force to slice the man's body almost in two. The samurai keeled over backwards in his saddle, his body trying to break at the spine. As he bent, intestines bulged forth and out over the front of his saddle to trail along the side of his wild-eyed horse.

The second rider was heading for Casca, his sword cutting wheels in the air as he closed on the barbarian thinking Casca was only another hairy Ainu tribesman from the northern lands. Casca had no trouble in his use of the *naginata* in locking the horns of the halberd on the blade of the samurai. A quick pull and a twist and the samurai's sword flew over his head to be lost in the mud of the rice paddy. Then Casca made a quick circular cross-blow that brought his broad blade snapping back to connect at the junction of the jaw and the samurai's throat rings. It was not a particularly heavy blow, but sufficient enough to open up the man's throat so he was well on his way to whatever heaven or hell he believed in. The horse reared as it came face to face with the barbarian standing on the bank of the dike and nearly sat on its haunches as it dropped its dying rider off its back. Leaping down from the dike, Casca moved to stand beside Muramasa as they faced the last of the enemy.

Sakai had observed the actions of his men against the two *ronin* with detachment. Obviously his vassals deserved to die if they could not take the heads of two such as these. They were of no import. He would attend to that small detail himself now that these two had proved themselves to be at least worthy of the effort of drawing his sword, *Willow Song*, from its sheath. He did, however, take notice of Muramasa's movements against his samurai. They were quick and skillful. He would do better to face this one on earth where his feet were solidly planted, for he was not known as a great horseman. As for the *gaijin*, he refused to let the odds of two against one bother him. He had dealt with greater odds before.

Muramasa motioned Casca back. His blood was singing a song of blood passion. *Well Drinker* was ready. They were as one, the shining steel and the master. And he the student who stood apart, detached from the action, he was the servant of the blade. Never had he felt so alive. He did not wish to share any of the blood with his big-nosed companion. There was even a slight sense of anger that the barbarian had taken one of his kills from him.

Sakai Taira was no mean swordsman as he had proved time and again over forty-three years of battles for the honor of his family. Stepping forward, he called to Muramasa, "Are you ready to die, slime from the gut of an *eta* whore?"

Muramasa bowed formally. Straightening, he brought *Well Drinker* up slowly, then instantly went

into an eye-splitting series of movements, slices, and
cuts. He never left his basic position: right foot
forward, body slightly leaning, his weight evenly
distributed with his center, strong, ready to move in
any direction as the *katana* danced in his hands,
catching the light of the afternoon sun.

"*Hai*, I am ready, are you, for this day another
Taira worm will feed the earth with his blood. Now
let us dance the dance of swords for the enlightenment of the *gaijin*."

Sakai felt his face flush with blood. Stepping
forward, he didn't wait, but went into a whirling
attack designed to break down his opponent's defense by forcing him to respond to each attack,
which would in the end leave him open for the
killing blow. The opening did not come. Two minutes passed and the *katana* of the *ronin* never wavered. The detestable scum laughed at his feeble
efforts, driving Sakai to greater fury in his attacks.

Muramasa laughed evilly and with great pleasure.
Half a dozen times he could have ended the contest.
No! *Well Drinker* could have ended it. But the game
had to be played a bit longer. Sometimes it was not
enough to simply kill. The opponent must be humili-
ated, ashamed. That made his death sweeter, and
Muramasa knew full well the shame in Sakai's soul,
to be beaten by a common soldier. If there had been
a way to stop the contest at this point, he had no
doubt that Sakai would have had to perform *seppuku*
to relieve his name of the dishonor being cast upon it

with each block and counterblow from the bandit with the shining sword.

Three minutes and Muramasa's arm felt as fresh as when the first blow was struck, but the strain was telling on Sakai. His face was florid and his movements were becoming slower and more awkward. The years of rich food and soft women instead of practice were taking their toll. He was going to die and now he knew it. Drawing back, he prepared himself for his final attack. From his *obi* he withdrew the companion to his *katana*, a shorter blade of something over a foot in length. Now that he had accepted his death, he would take this laughing *ronin* with him. A calmness pulled the blood back from his face. The trembling in his arms ceased as he regained control of his breathing, sucking the air deep into his lower abdomen. Muramasa knew what was taking place. Sakai was committing himself to death at this moment.

Casca also sensed that the game was about to reach its finale.

CHAPTER SIX

Resting his weight on the haft of the *naginata*, Casca concentrated on the fight, if it could be called that. It was obvious from the opening moves that Sakai was seriously outmatched and Muramasa was toying with him. What he had seen Muramasa do in the past was nothing compared to the lesson he was giving the samurai lord. Muramasa began to surgically dismantle Sakai, cutting his expensive robes into ribbons, barely touching the flesh beneath. He cut only enough to open the skin so it would bleed but never enough to maim or kill.

Sakai halted, drew back, and removed his mask. Beneath it his face was a combination of red flushed skin and white lips. He sucked in breath to feed his burning lungs. Muramasa gave him his chance to take in fresh air. And then he moved, this time with a difference. The game was over; now it was time to kill. And kill he did. Before Sakai could counter, his sword arm was taken off at the elbow, leaving him his shorter blade in his left hand. Then it, too, was on the earth. Sakai dropped to his knees, staring at his bloody stumps. He had only seconds to live and knew it. Raising his eyes to Muramasa, he pleaded without saying a word and leaned forward, extending his neck out. *Well Drinker* whistled through the air and Sakai's head rolled free of its body.

Muramasa stood back from the body of his victim, eyes red with blood passion, chest heaving, sweat rolling freely down his face and arms. It was, again, beyond sexual experience. He knew he was close to the edge of some unknown nirvana. Casca's wondering eyes were ignored. If the *gaijin* had come to him at that time, he might have turned *Well Drinker* on him.

Casca could feel the vibrations transmitting from Muramasa. Instinctively he waited for the trembling to pass and his breathing to return to normal. Then and only then did he speak. "We go now?"

Muramasa turned to stare at the unexpected voice that had interrupted his thoughts. It took a moment for it to register. Then his eyes cleared, the fog lifting from them.

"*Hai*. We go."

Casca rounded up the horses. They had lost one but that left them two including the fine bay gelding Sakai had been riding. After stripping the bodies of goods and weapons, they were quite well outfitted. Casca tossed the naked bodies over the side of the ditch. That might give them a little time before someone found the remains and a search for the killers was started. Mounted on the saddles were *zutsu* cases with Mongol-style laminated bows and shafts in them. Obviously the retainers of Lord Sakai had not deigned them worth killing by arrows.

After tossing the last body over, Casca finished packing their goods in the saddlebags and tied down what was loose where he could. Like the deceased and mutilated Sakai, he was not a great horseman, though the gods alone knew how many thousands of leagues he had ridden on the back of a horse over the centuries. The only thing he liked about them was that he knew they would save a lot of time wherever they were going and give his feet a rest while he built up callouses on his ass. Settling into the saddle, he waited for the sword maker.

Muramasa shook his head as he looked at the remains of Sakai. It was a shame; the fine robes of silk were so cut up and bloody. They had been of great value. Just the outer robe was worth enough to feed a peasant family for two years.

With a sigh of regret, Muramasa swung up into the saddle of Sakai's animal. As for the clothes, as always he had taken the best. Once he had looked closely at Casca to see if this had caused the barbarian any concern. Obviously it had not, or perhaps he was just not able to read the face of this strange *gaijin*. To his eyes, they all looked very much alike— ugly. Turning his animal's head back the way they had come, Muramasa led them back up the trail into the mountains. Now that they had killed Sakai and his vassals, there would sooner or later be a hue and cry for them. The farther away they were by then the better. If they could make it to where one of the

supporters of Yoritomo was in power, then they
would have a chance.

The swords they brought with them of the dead
vassals of the Taira and their master would be their
passports to honor and employment in the forces of
the Minamoto—which would bring Muramasa that
much closer to his heart's desire. He would be samurai. Perhaps even one day he would be *daimyo*, a
great land owner with many *koku* of rice granted to
him each year by Lord Yoritomo. It was good to
have dreams, for what was one without them? And
then when he had the right to the *dai-sho*, he would
complete what he had begun at the spring of his
fathers. When he had forged *Well Drinker*, he had
not made a companion blade, for the temptation to
carry it as *dai-sho* would then have been too much.

When he was truly samurai, then he would forge
the little brother to *Well Drinker*. The thought chilled
him that the companion to *Well Drinker* might also
have the same powers. He shook the thought away
from him as a dog threw water from its pelt. No!
That could not happen. It would be impossible for
the elements to be brought together again in the
same manner.

It was dark by the time they had reached the spot
where earlier in the day Muramasa had made up his
mind to go down into the lowlands. He didn't have
to try and explain to Casca the reason for his change
of mind. Both men felt more secure, if not as warm,
with the choice of paths. Muramasa led the way
through groves of elm and pine, often dismounting

to rest his horse as well as his own buttocks. He took
them on narrow tree-shrouded paths that grew darker
by the moment as the sun goddess, Ameratsu, sank
into the burning sea.

When at last total darkness forced them to call a
halt to their travel, it was with relief that both men
gathered soft ferns with which to make their beds for
the night around a small sheltered campfire.

Casca was tired and knew that Muramasa had to
be emotionally drained, though he made no complaint nor showed any overt sign of it. But Casca
knew by the small lines at the corners of his eyes
and the way the mouth and shoulders set that the
man was exhausted. Shaking his head in confusion,
he knew only one thing for certain, that life around
Muramasa was always very exciting. In the short
time he had known him, they had killed seven men.
He had the uneasy feeling that that was just the
introduction to whatever play Muramasa had in mind.

Muramasa was indeed tired, but he could make no
complaint, nor show any sign of weakness. That was
not permitted. Leaning on his elbow, he glanced at
the barbarian Casca. What did he think of the events
of the past weeks? The scarred man was not unlike
himself in many ways. He never complained and was
certainly a fierce fighter, though his style was a bit
crude and in need of refinement. All he had been
able to find out was that he had come from far away
and was not a member of the tribe of pale red
creatures who lived north in the farthermost part of
Honshu and Hokkaido, the people called the Ainu.

What could he tell this *gaijin* that might make him
understand of the terrible hunger within his soul to
be samurai. To wear the *dai-sho* in his own right, to
have sons after him who would be samurai. How
could this large gray-eyed animal know that in these
sacred islands of the gods only the samurai were
human? Yet he knew that was not right. He felt, he
hungered, and he had pride, but he was not samurai.
And now he had this other *kami*—or was it *iki-ryo*?—an evil spirit, riding him. *Well Drinker*, what
had he done to deserve such a karma? To be bur-
dened with a large ugly barbarian and a cursed sword.
Aiie! It was too much for him. He would find a
shrine and speak to the wise men there. Until then
all was in the hands of the gods, all homage to
Amida Bhudda.

At dawn they fed from the rations the vassals of
Sakai had carried with them, sticky rice with pieces of
dried, smoked fish and strands of gray-yellow seaweed for flavoring.

Muramasa smacked his lips over the meal. Casca
wanted to kill something and get a piece of meat
down his gut. He had never understood how a people, those of Chin included, could be so warlike on a
vegetable diet. He needed some red meat or at least
some fowl of one kind or another. After what he
thought was a meager breakfast, with little if any
flavor, they saddled back up and headed out on the
mountain trail. The day was crisp with the high
morning mist that rested on the tops of the moun-

tains, then slid down into the valleys and lowlands before being burned off by the new sun.

The trail narrowed even more as they passed over one mountain range, then another. At clearings along the way, Muramasa would halt and point off into the distance at a village or castle, telling Casca who controlled it. Then he would tell him who was *daimyo* of the lands they were crossing, which Muramasa explained meant great landowner. So far none of the names had brought anything to Muramasa's lips except anger.

It looked as if the Taira were the bosses of most of this area. Casca wondered when they would reach the first stronghold where Yoritomo Minamoto had followers. He hoped it would be soon. Several times Muramasa tried to explain to him the relationships between the great warring families and their god-king who lived in a great palace in the city of Heian-Kyo, somewhere near a mountain called Hiei. None of it made any sense to Casca, but he listened intently, each time picking up another word or two. One day what Muramasa was telling him might be of value.

When at last they came off the mountains and into the lowlands once more, he could see they were at a narrow strait separating the island they were on from another. Here it grew more crowded as they passed through village after village. There was no way to avoid them. All the surrounding land was used in farming the fields of rice. If they had gotten off the road, they would have had to trek through miles of soggy, stinking rice paddies. As usual, Casca drew

the most attention, not only because of his size and
coloring, but because of the robes he was wearing,
ones he'd taken from one of the slain samurai of
Lord Sakai Taira. They were the Taira colors but he
certainly did not have the look of the samurai of the
lands of the Sun Goddess.

Casca was as curious as they were. Several times
he saw women moving daintily along the streets,
their feet clad in white *tabi* resting on wooden san-
dals with two high ridges on the bottoms to keep the
wearer's feet from the dirt and mud. These women
had faces covered in masks of thick white powder
and the most elaborate hairstyles he'd ever seen.
Their robes were costly and of many colors, one
color overlaying the other in eye-pleasing patterns
as the women minced and bowed their way along the
streets, hiding their faces behind gaily painted fans.
Several of them eyed Muramasa with obvious speculation since he was well-dressed and riding a fine
horse. As to the barbarian behind him, he hardly
entered their thoughts, and if he did, it was no more
than idle speculation of how unpleasant it must be to
pillow with one so large and so ugly.

They let their animals do the hard work and push
their way through the throngs. Fishermen from the
sea were hawking their early-morning catch, conical
straw hats and capes over weathered shoulders and
bent backs. Street stalls with pots of steaming noo-
dles and vegetables were everywhere. Casca's mouth
watered when he saw a cage filled with pigeons, but
Muramasa had his mind on something else: getting

across the Straits of Shimonoseki to the island of Honshu where he could find supporters of Lord Yoritomo. Only there could they find sanctuary. Every second spent on Kyushu was a second of danger where they might be questioned. If that happened and the packs on their animals were inspected, they were surely doomed to a most unpleasant death. For in their packs were the swords and accoutrements of the Taira samurai they had killed.

As they neared the waterfront, Muramasa stopped and spoke briefly to a fisherman who refused to look directly up at the face of the horseman as he spoke in a quick, frightened burst. He pointed with a black-nailed, calloused finger down a cobblestone alleyway running between houses of bamboo set off the ground. Between them were strung lines on which all types of fish were hung out to dry in the sun. Aromatic!

At the end of the street, they found themselves at the edge of the sea. The tide was just beginning to turn. Resting in slimy, fish-head-littered mud was a flat-bottomed boat with one mast. Casca figured that Muramasa was going to hire the boat, not wishing to take one of the others that regularly carried passengers and cargo to Honshu. He obviously wanted to avoid contact with any of Taira's men.

CHAPTER SEVEN

The ritual haggling did not take very long. The look in Muramasa's eyes when he touched the hilt of *Well Drinker* made the bargemen come to a rapid agreement. Laying down weathered, half-soaked planks, he led their horses aboard the flat-bottomed boat, explaining with much bowing and scraping that it would be half an hour before the tide was in enough to float the contraption off the mud banks. Muramasa puffed out his cheeks at the delay as if it were the personal fault of the bargeman that the tide wasn't ready at the same time he was.

Casca noticed the anxious look in Muramasa's eyes as he kept glancing to the shore and the alley-way leading to their water-logged barge.

The *ronin* was very concerned. He had no doubt that word of the two strangers' entry into the city would be rapidly passed to the *shugo*, constables, samurai police of the Taira. Every breath he took might be bringing him closer to death. Death he did not mind. It was natural, expected. But to die before achieving his goals—that was a thought which was

63

unbearable. Even with *Well Drinker* in his hand, one could only resist so many opponents before he had to fall.

The incoming tide lapped slowly, sluggishly, brown and filthy against the unpainted, weathered sides of the barge. Inch by dragging inch it slowly applied lift against the soaked hull. Whistling under his breath to attract Muramasa's attention, Casca pointed down the alleyway. Coming to stand beside him hand on hilt, Muramasa squinted his eyes to see better in the reflected glare of the sunlight on the murky waters.

Two women were approaching them. One wore a wide-brimmed hat with black woven strands of cotton hanging down to conceal much of her features and protect her face from the rays of the sun. The other was obviously of the servant class and trotted behind her mistress carrying two large bundles, one on her back and the other under a fleshy arm. She was of no interest, being short, plain and very fat. But the other was of definite interest. As Muramasa had often stated, he was cursed with great curiosity. She moved with rapid yet dainty steps that bespoke a lady of quality or perhaps a woman of the Willow World, such as they had passed earlier in the streets.

Casca stood back as Muramasa advanced to the plank walkway to greet the woman and her companion as they stopped at the water's edge and waited.

Muramasa didn't feel very sure of himself when dealing with ladies of quality. Men were something different. Highborn or low, the *katana* was the final judge when you met one on one. But with a woman, who knew what the contest really was?

"You wish something, mistress?"

The woman's voice was not low or high. It stayed in the middle range but was very melodic. She bowed, her face still hidden for the most part by the hanging strands of black cotton dangling from her wide-brimmed straw hat.

"Indeed, honorable sir. I wish to join you and your associate and cross to the mainland. Is it possible that you would grant a desperate and defenseless woman and her companion the honor of accompanying you?" She bowed deeper. Her form was graceful, studied, as was the manner of her speech. It was not the voice of a woman of rural origins. She used phraseology and accents of the highborn. But of which family?

Before he had an opportunity to reply, Casca whistled at him again, this time more loudly and with a feeling of urgency to the pitch. Coming down the alley, two abreast, were four mounted horsemen. Behind them came six men on foot, all wearing the *dai-sho*. They were samurai, most probably *shugo*, police of the local Taira *daimyo*.

The woman heard the muffled clatter of the horses' hooves as they trampled through the muddy street. Instantly her body took on the signals of fear. Muramasa made his mind up. It made no difference if the horsemen were coming after the woman or not. If they were, then they would still be certain to question him and Casca. Therefore, it was quite simple to make his decision.

"Of course. But if you wish to come aboard, may I suggest that you do so quickly." He glanced at the water level. Only an inch or two more to go and they should be able to float free. As the *shugo* neared them, Muramasa ordered the bargeman to make ready with his long pole to push them out. He started to call out an order to Casca, then saw the barbarian was already prepared, having taken one of the Mongol-style bows from its case. He had already notched a shaft and was waiting. Muramasa grunted under his breath. From the manner in which the long nose held the bow, it was obvious he knew something about its use. Perhaps he was not going to be such a burden after all.

The women hurried aboard, moving to the rear of the barge behind the horses. The bargeman looked as if he wished to abandon ship, but the big barbarian with the scarred face indicated with his bow that if he made such a move, the first shaft would be for him. He had no choice but to stay and do as he was ordered by these, what he now believed to be, out-law *ronin*.

Knowing they had no other options and seeing that it would be incredibly foolish to let the advancing *shugo* get any nearer, Muramasa nodded at Casca and waited to observe the quality of the barbarian's marksmanship. Casca raised the bow, holding the string by an ivory thumbgrip next to his ear. Then he extended the powerful laminated bow forward with his left hand, bringing it down from above his head to eye level in one smooth motion as he completed the draw. Then the arrow was released, leaving the string of the bow humming. The first shaft hit its mark, the leading horse, in the chest. The shaft penetrated into the lungs. The beast screamed like a wounded woman and fell to its forelegs, kicking and screaming as its mouth filled with blood. The rider went over its head to crash in the alley and lay motionless. With any luck, he broke his neck.

The next shaft was in the air before the first rider touched the earth. This one struck the second rider in the chest, penetrating his lacquered armor in the style of *dhotoke-do*, a shining black human chest. The arrow was driven with enough force that the barbed point protruded out his back. He fell over his horse's neck, trying to hold on as his lungs filled with blood. His horse ran into the flailing legs of the leading animal who screamed and writhed on the earth in its death spasms. Its hind legs kicked out and knocked the second horse down.

Behind them, the samurai on foot paused in confusion. They wanted to attack, but the horses in front of them were screaming and kicking so much that none wished to venture near and risk a broken limb.

Muramasa admired the barbarian's logic in the selection of his targets. Quite good. Pushing the gangway free with his foot, he drew *Well Drinker* and waited. Not looking back, he barked harshly at the bargeman, "If this thing does not move soon, you are going to die. For if we do not kill you," he

pointed at the samurai who had finally found their
way around the kicking and dying horses, "then
they will!"

The bargeman found new strength in his ancient
frame as he dug the pole deeper into the mud, his
tendons stretched to the breaking point in his neck
and back as he shoved against the sucking slime. He
thought he felt the barge give an inch or two and
pushed harder until he thought his heart was going to
burst.

Casca let loose three more arrows, only one of
which struck its mark as the on-rushing samurai
were dodging and weaving. But he did have the
satisfaction of hearing one scream as the man went
down with a shaft of the leaf pattern stuck deep in
his leg, the tip just touching the deep artery in the
thigh. The samurai didn't know it, but the first time
he got up and tried to move or pull the shaft out, he
would bleed to death.

Slowly the barge began to inch out into the slimy
water. Muramasa studiously ignored the women who
had taken cover behind the horses, but he did not fail
to notice that the lady in the hat had a *namban-bo*, a
chisel-edged knife, in her delicate hand and stood
ready. *Well Drinker* was beginning to hum in his
hand, sending the now familiar, and at the same time
welcome and dreaded, vibrations up his arm at the
prospect of blood.

The three *shugo* did not hesitate when they reached
the edge of the water. They leaped in full stride to
reach the decks of the slowly retreating barge. *Well*

Drinker hummed in the air, catching one of the samurai with a *junmoji*, a crosswise cut, while he was still in the air. The effect was quite interesting for Muramasa as he had never seen the cut made in that fashion before. It sliced the man from the left lower hip to his right clavical, splitting him open. His body collapsed in midair as though the spring in his leap was suddenly removed. He fell half on the deck.

The other two made the crossing. Casca met one with his sword, blocking the man's first cut in an arm-jarring counter. His opponent's blade flashed in front of his face, nearly giving him a mate to the scar he already wore.

By all the gods of hades! These small bastards are fast, he thought.

Knowing the man was quicker than he was, he did the only logical thing—something illogical. He threw his weapon straight at the samurai's grinning face. Instinctively, the man had to duck, blink, and block all at the same time. When his eyes opened, Casca had his sword wrist in one hand and his other arm around his back, twisting both. The samurai's arm came loose first at the shoulder as the sockets separated. Releasing his grip on the now useless and empty sword arm, Casca transferred his grip to the man's head. Grasping the samurai's topknot in his hand, he held the body rigid as he twisted, turning the man's head to an impossible angle. It gave way. The neck cracked at the sixth vertebra. Casca let the body slide over the side. His man was done. Picking up his *katana* where it had fallen to the deck after being blocked by a frantic wave of the dead samurai's sword, he turned to see if Muramasa needed any help. He saw he was wasting his concern. The last samurai was half kneeling, his head split open to the chest, the two halves pulling apart with a distinct sucking sound. Then *Well Drinker* rose and fell again, completing the halving process. Muramasa cut the man in two parts from head to groin.

Muramasa groaned in pleasure. The feel of the cut was so . . . so perfect. The feeling of the steel slicing through flesh and bone was not to be equaled by any other sensation. Raising the bloody steel above his head, he marveled at the beauty of the contrasting colors of the watered steel blending in a thousand different shades with the blood as the light of the sun reflected off the blade. It was glorious. Each time he drew *Well Drinker* to fight, it was *shini-mono-gurui*, the exalted "Hour of the Death Fury," when nothing can touch you save death, and that has no importance.

"Ikaga desu ka?" Casca asked, careful to keep his distance from Muramasa while he held *Well Drinker*. He didn't know just what it was, but when Muramasa had the sword in his hand and had killed, there was something different about him and it wasn't good.

Carefully wiping the blood from *Well Drinker* with a silk scarf, Muramasa replied quite pleasantly, amused at Casca's use of his few words in the human tongue. "I am quite well, *domo arigato*."

A movement in the rear of the barge caught his eye. He had forgotten about the women. The woman in the hat placed her *namban-bo* back in her robes and bowed gracefully to him. Her servant was in a near state of shock, as was the bargeman.

To the bargeman, Muramasa barked roughly, "Get us out of here and raise the sail. I do not wish to spend any more time on this unclean device than is necessary."

The bargeman made no verbal response, but if he had, he would have replied in the same manner that he wanted them off his boat as fast as possible. He was not certain in his mind that he was not going to lose his head anyway, for the samurai of Taira had been killed on his property. Miserable, he railed at his misfortune and did as he was ordered. Raising his single tattered sail of rattan, he made for the Straits of Shimonoseki and the main island of Honshu, where, if Amida Bhudda was kind, he would put off these people with their swords and never see them again.

CHAPTER EIGHT

The Lady Yoshiko no Hirimoto bowed to the *ronin* with sincere respect. Although she was samurai, never had she seen sword dance such as she had just witnessed. The man might not be of her class, but he was without a doubt a warrior to be reckoned with. And there was his strange companion who had killed the samurai by snapping his neck as if it were no more than a rotten twig. Such strength, though certainly there was a certain lack of finesse to his technique.

Her maid began to whimper. Quickly she corrected her. "Quiet, remember who you serve! We are samurai. Never let common people see you with weakness!"

Yoshiko was absolutely sincere. If the *ronin* had not been able to dispose of the *shugo*, she would have killed herself before permitting them to take her captive. She could not let her life be used to threaten her family. Her delicate, well-groomed manner covered a heart as fierce as any of her family. Samurai women had their duty also, even to the death.

Perhaps these men might be of service to her, for she had far to go and alone it would be difficult. Even more important, they had horses.

As the gray-eyed big man was obviously a barbarian, she felt no need to address herself to him.

"May I ask as to the name of our rescuer and most humbly apologize for being the instrument by which you have become involved with our problems?" She removed her hat.

Casca felt his chest clench. Her face was bare of the white powder of the women he had seen earlier. Her complexion was very pale gold with roses and milk for accent. Her hair was set high on her head, bundled loosely under her straw hat. She was without question one of the most beautiful and exotic women he had ever seen in all his years of wandering.

Muramasa felt his face flush with awkward emotion. This was the first time in his life that a high-born had ever spoken to him as if he were a true man and not just another peasant soldier to be thrown away like so much chaff before the winnowing winds of war.

Trying to affect the more refined speech of the nobles he answered stiffly, "I am Jinto Muramasa, my lady. May I inquire as to your name?" He bowed deeply with respect.

Gracefully she responded in kind, inclining her head delicately, showing the nape of her neck to be as long and graceful as the swans that swam in the lily ponds of the Emperor's palace at Heian-Kyo. "With pleasure, good sir. And may I say that your name, War Sword, is most apt." She knew now that he had killed samurai of the Taira, he could not betray her to them without losing his own head. She said demurely, "I am Yoshiko no Hirimoto."

"Ahhh!" He hissed between his teeth. So that was it. Her father, Oe no Hirimoto, was known to be a noble and an important advisor to the Minamoto. If she could be taken hostage, it would be very difficult for her family, even if she was never ransomed or set free. The *shugo* were after her.

Casca coughed politely. He didn't know what was going on, but he didn't want to be left out of this. Let Muramasa take his pick of horses and clothes, but this was something different.

Muramasa frowned at his companion's ill manner, but he felt he did owe him at least an introduction to a great lady of a noble house. It would further his education greatly. Bowing again, he asked, "If it would not offend you, Yoshiko no Hirimoto-san, I would like to present my traveling companion. He is a most curious man, but as you have just witnessed, sometimes a most useful person."

She smiled at the big pale man as she would one of her father's pet dogs. She had never seen anything like him. He was so ugly that he was almost attractive in a perverted way. Her face flushed at such an indelicate thought.

"Is he an Ainu?"

"No, my lady, he is from somewhere else, very far away. That is all I have been able to find out about him. He comes from beyond the lands of the great Khan. He is called Casca-san."

Casca bowed at the mention of his name, but he never took his eyes off the woman called Yoshiko. Politely, but not too politely as she remembered her position, she said, *"Domo arigato gozai mashte.* I thank you Casca-san for your aid this day." Looking at Muramasa, she continued, "I assure you that my family will be most appreciative of your valuable services to them this day and in the days to come."

Muramasa knew she was sucking him in and didn't mind it. His karma was good this day. She was the daughter of Oe no Hirimoto, a most important supporter of Yoritomo Minamoto in their struggle with the Taira. Most important. This *onna*, woman, could be their admission to the highborn Minamotos, where they would be noticed and rewarded for their services to her. Ahh yes. He was most pleased for the opportunity to render this lady his services. For now it would be best if they said nothing of their own problems with the Taira.

"Ah so desu, Yoshiko-san. I feel the gods have brought us together so that I may be of service to you. For I have long served the cause of the Minamoto against the tyrant Taira. It will be a great honor for such poor men as we to be of service to the daughter of Oe no Hirimoto. We," he indicated Casca, "will see to you and your servant's safety to the extent of our lives."

Casca didn't have the faintest idea of what Muramasa was getting them into and wouldn't have argued about it anyway. As was their now normal practice, they stripped the bodies naked and pushed them over the side, after taking what they wished and stuffing it into their packs. The women did not seem to be the least bit embarrassed at the sight of naked dead men. A tough race! Even the flowers, Casca thought, have thorns.

The crossing was an easy one. The bargeman tacked back and forth with practiced skills from his long years of making this crossing every day, the weather permitting. It was two hours before nightfall when they made land on the island of Honshu. In the event that word of their flight from Kyushu had been sent by carrier pigeon or some other means, Muramasa had the bargeman maneuver them a bit to the east where they would not have to go through any villages immediately.

Leading the horses ashore, they gave up their seats to the women, knowing they would make better time. Yoshiko rode well, although her maid tended to wobble a bit even when the horse was standing still. Muramasa took the reins of Yoshiko's borrowed horse and called back to Casca, "*Isogi*, we must hurry!" Then he took off without another look back.

The bargeman looked at the three silver coins in his hand with relief. He had been certain that he would not live to see another day brought to glory by the sacred light of Ameratsu. Perhaps his karma would carry him through the next days in safety, especially if he did not push it too much and stayed out of sight for a month or two. That thought did not displease him greatly. His wife was famous for having a sharp and unforgiving tongue.

Muramasa led the way, taking them along several different winding trails but always leading them to the north. It was four hours after landing when Lady Yoshiko finally pleaded with him, *"Dozo ga matsu."*

Muramasa was glad that she had called for a halt first. He was growing weary, but it would have been unseemly for him to admit it without losing face in front of the lady and the barbarian. One must always set the example as well as the pace.

That night they pulled off the trail to take shelter in a glen surrounded by high willows. Beside the tallest willow rested a small stone shrine spotted with greenish-white lichens with signs of recent offerings on the small pedestal at its base. All but Casca bowed respectfully when they first neared the shrine. But then they paid no further attention to it.

He and Muramasa took turns on guard, letting the women catch their sleep. They would probably have need of it in the coming days. He and Muramasa talked for a few moments, Casca adding to his list of words and phrases while Muramasa shook his head in disbelief at the half-understood tales Casca told him of the outside world. He told him of the great cities of the Genghis, of Rome and the legions, Byzantium and Sarmatia, and Persia and the Vandals. It was too much for Muramasa to believe that anywhere in the world there could be a greater or richer city than that of the Son of Heaven, who, though just a boy of eight years, was still by divine right a direct descendant from the immortal gods. Ahhh, surely, this long-nosed ugly one was a great storyteller and was simply trying to be amusing in his clumsy fashion.

Through the night, they took their turns, letting the coals of the fire die down after they had eaten. There was no sense in advertising their presence if it could be avoided. Muramasa took first watch, using the time to set the scale of his life and future in balance. He knew that he had failed in many things, but now he had the chance to succeed. Or did he? Was what to become of him now more in the length of the cold shining steel he called *Well Drinker* than himself? Would it one day drink from his blood also?

Ahhh, well, if it did, then that, too, was his karma. Until then he would play the great game against all who came. It had been a most unusual series of events that had happened to him since he had found the long-nosed one on the beach. Perhaps he was a spirit form or possibly he was possessed by one. The scars on his knotted body were enough to give one nightmares. Muramasa was a warrior and knew the meaning of many of those wounds he had seen. The man should have died several times over or at the least have been a pathetic cripple with amputated limbs. Perhaps the gods were keeping him alive to do their bidding and somehow aid Muramasa to realize his ambitions.

CHAPTER NINE

Eyes watched the *ronin* by the shrine several times during the night, though not the eyes of bandits or samurai of the Taira. They were the eyes of Yoshiko no Hirimoto. She slept as a warrior did. Every sound, no matter how slight, was instantly registered. When one was not identified by the subconscious, her eyes would instantly snap open as her hand tightened on the handle of the *namban-bo*. When she did wake, there were always doubts about her fortune to nag her. Was she lucky to be in the company of two such as these? They did look disreputable and the big barbarian was frightening in the extreme by his very difference.

But they had killed the Taira, that was not in doubt. And what would her chances be to reach Kamakura without them? There were still many days to go, and her chances of making it without an escort were very slim indeed. She had to make it. Much depended on her reaching Kamakura. From there her message could be sent directly and safely to Yoritomo.

Aiie, it would be good when she could put

down the weight of her responsibility. For now only she was free and able to bring Yoritomo the information that the Kwanto was his when he was ready to move against the Taira. The passes leading to and from the eight provinces would be controlled by those who would rally to him once he was in position to threaten and take Heian-Kyo—if he made it that far. First he would have many battles to fight and win before he advanced to the Kwanto. But if he did, then he would not be resisted and the passes to the city of the Emperor would be open to him, as well as having at least three of the most powerful barons of the Kwanto throw their forces in with his.

If she did not manage to get the message to Yoritomo, then who could say what alignments might occur if he did not move rapidly enough to secure the fealty of the lords of the Kwanto now that it was proffered. If he hesitated, they could change their minds, and the passes would be closed to him. He might, it was true, go around or come in from the south. But to do so would cost him more men than he could comfortably spare.

There were at this time no alternatives. She had to concentrate on one day at a time. The farther north they went, the safer they were. Here in Suo Province they were in constant danger. The spies and scouts of Taira would be looking for her on all roads and paths. They knew she carried a message of great import that could change the course of the war. Just what it was, they did not know and would without the slightest hesitation kill thousands if need be to find out. That was all the torturers of Munemori no Taira, brother to Shigimori, could find out from her mother before she died. That was all she knew. It was a great sadness that her mother had not found the courage to take her own life when the soldiers of Taira came for her. She would have saved herself great pain and not have put her family in jeopardy. Yoshiko hoped that her uncle would be able to have proper funeral rites performed for her spirit so that it might rest.

First light found the small party taking the ridge trail from Suo to Akia, then on to Bitchu where Yoshiko said they might find aid from a relative of her family. That would be welcome news for all. They were running short of everything. Food would be needed soon, and to go into any of the villages was to invite disaster. For Muramasa and Casca were certain that by now the Taira would be after them with a vengeance, and their descriptions, especially Casca's, would surely doom them if he was seen.

To counter this as best he could, Casca took to wearing a scarf tied tightly about his head to conceal his hair and tried as much as possible to keep his features from casual view. He hid them under a wide-brimmed straw hat he had picked up when a traveling farmer saw the party approach and ran away rather than meet them, leaving his hat behind.

He and Muramasa each led one of the animals. Returning the better clothes they had taken from the dead to their packs, they tried to look as much like simple porters and servants as they could. Each kept his weapons close to hand, for they both felt that somewhere on the road, if their luck held true, they would have need of them again. Casca did regret having to leave the *naginata* behind at their last stop, but there was no way to conceal it among their goods. But they did have their bows if they had time to get them out and in use.

Wishing they were able, even for a short time, to visit some of the cities they passed on the way, Casca reconciled himself to trying to remain as anonymous as possible. It wasn't easy. He was much larger and broader than most of the native population and would stand out in any crowd. He had heard the people of Chin refer to the inhabitants of these islands as dwarfs. That was not exactly true. There were some they'd met, as he had found among the samurai, who were taller and heavier boned. It was probably diet. As usual, nobles ate much better than the people who grew the food for them.

Their first two days travel on Honshu were uneventful except for the whining of the maid who saw swords in every shadow. She wished fervently that she had stayed in her home fishing village and had married the old man who had asked her father for her. By now he would be dead and she would be the owner of two fine boats instead of on this terrible journey with these barbarians and savages who might ravish her and her mistress. Tears came to her eyes when she thought of the humiliation, but also a warming to her loins.

Near noon they ran into their first stroke of bad luck—six men on foot wearing the colors of Taira. Only one was samurai, the others common soldiers with poor weapons and simple breastplates of lacquered wood for armor.

Casca tried to shrink and make himself smaller as he moved closer to the rear of the horse with the maid mounted on it, his hand unobtrusively moving near the concealed handle of his sword among their packs. Muramasa did the same. Acting startled and frightened by the presence of soldiers, he bowed his way to the rear of his horse where *Well Drinker* lay in wait.

Casca had a feeling that they might have a remote chance to get away if Muramasa kept the sword in its sheath. Every time he drew the thing, killing started. He wished he knew what it was about the blade that had frightened old Hama-san and driven him out of their camp so fast. That there was something, he had no doubt, but Muramasa had not spoken to him of it, and he didn't know how to ask properly.

The samurai in charge of the patrol was a broad-shouldered, bow-legged man with good, if not expensive, robes. He raised his hand in front of them, calling both the travelers and his soldiers to a halt.

Striding forward a few paces in front of his men, he tried to peer under the broad-brimmed tasseled hat of the woman on horseback. His eyes missed nothing. He took his time before addressing her, noting the manner in which she held her body, the carefully tended nails of her hands. Everything about her said this was a lady of quality. He was looking for a lady with another older woman and two men who were fierce fighters. All looked to be such, except the men were not so very dangerous-looking to his eyes. They kowtowed and backed away, bowing in subservience as was their due, something no true warrior would do. But the lady was the mystery.

Unless they were on some errand requiring secrecy, they would have traveled the main roads, which were much safer and patrolled by the warriors of Taira who kept the order and drove the bandits into these very hills. That the woman was here was most suspicious. But there could be another answer. He hoped for such. The woman beneath the tasseled hat was very beautiful.

Casca could see the glint of lust in the shave-pated samurai's eyes, which was why he hoped once more that wishful thinking would overrule intelligence.

With the automatic contempt his class held for those beneath them, he ignored the two porters, giving them hardly a glance. That they were obviously cowed was normal. No mere serf would dare to raise his eyes to a samurai without permission. These two did everything except urinate down their legs. That he also took as his due, for he was indeed a most fearsome and powerful warrior.

Peasants should be frightened of him. Twice he had performed *tsujugiri* in the streets of his city.

This he did not do randomly but waited for one who offended him by his manners or lack of them. Only then did he test the new sword blade on the body of the offender.

"Greeting, lady. I am Jochiku Murakami, captain of guards, and I care for those who travel these trails and roads. May I inquire as to your name and destination?" He bowed politely, keeping his spine straight to show his martial spirit, his attention locked on the dark eyes with such incredibly long lashes that looked at him with certain interest. A chill of iced fire raced down from his stomach into his loins. It had been long since he had pillowed with a lady of quality, especially one with such bold eyes.

It was obvious that he impressed her greatly by the manner in which she moved her head so that the nape of her long graceful neck was best exposed to his view when she returned his bow from her saddle. His pulse raced as he came closer to her sword hand touching the reins of her horse. His soldiers stayed back. They would not come closer until they were bidden. He had always insisted on great discipline among his lessers. All should know their place in the structure of life at all times.

He was prepared to make the gentle opening moves of offering his protection for part of her journey when the spell of her eyes was broken by a hysterical sob from the maid. The tension was too much for her. Her bowels let loose as the samurai neared her lady. She couldn't control herself. A wail started from deep inside and broke out of her open mouth, startling the jays in the tops of the pine trees.

Before Casca or Muramasa could draw their swords from out of the pack, Yoshiko had already drawn her dagger and plunged the chiseled point straight into the officer's right eye. The razor-sharp tip cut easily through the bone in the occipital orb to reach the softer brain tissue behind. Jochiku Murakami's jerking head nearly twisted the knife out of her hand as he died.

Muramasa had *Well Drinker* out first and was rushing toward the startled soldiers when Casca came up close behind him. Yoshiko turned her horse off the trail to give them fighting room.

The common soldiers of Jochiku did not share the samurai view of noble death. Without him to lash them on, they had little taste for combat. Most of their efforts were in trying to get enough room to get away and run for help.

Muramasa took two of them, slicing the hardwood haft of one's *naginata* in twain with the same stroke that took the rest of his arm off at the shoulder. Then, whipping around, he dodged under a half-hearted thrust of a second soldier and sank *Well Drinker* deep into the man's armpit. Twisting the hungry blade to free it, he was going for the next one when Casca caught up to him in time to block a sideways slice of one of the long spears. Blocking the thrust with his sword, he stepped close inside to where the spear was nearly useless. Keeping the pressure on the haft of the spear, he smashed the man in the groin with a full swing of his knee and cut his throat as he fell to the earth, holding his crotch with anguished hands.

The other two took off with Muramasa in hot pursuit. He called back to Casca to remain with the women and guard them until he returned, then disappeared through a cluster of pines as he went after the soldiers. Casca did as he was bade and turned to go back to Yoshiko and the maid. Stopping in his tracks, he saw the maid lying on the side of the trail, her throat cut. Looking around quickly for the enemy they had missed, it took him a second to see the knife in Yoshiko's dainty hand. She had cut the throat of her maid.

Seeing Casca's distress, Yoshiko bowed her head in deep sorrow.

"*Ah so desu*, Casca-san. There are many sad duties in life. This has been one of them. I have known Tamiko-chan," she said with the term of endearment, "for many years. However she was a danger to us all and I could not permit the risk of her losing control again. It was most regrettable but most necessary. I am so sorry." A tear gathered at the corner of her eye that she gracefully took away with the tip of a flowered kerchief.

Casca felt a lump in his throat. He was right. The women of these islands were very dangerous butterflies.

CHAPTER TEN

It was nearly half an hour before Muramasa returned, bearing a grisly package of two human heads. He held them by the hair with one hand and *Well Drinker* clean and shining in the other.

"I brought these back so you would not fear that they had escaped to spread the word of our presence."

It was then he noticed the dead maid, in the bushes off to the side of the road where Casca had dragged her with the other corpses. He planned to move them to where they'd be out of sight and smell for a time.

Casca pointed to Yoshiko in response to Muramasa's unasked question. Grunting, Muramasa nodded his head in approval. "It is well. She will trouble us no further. If the *goke'nin* of Taira are looking for a young woman with two males and one female companion, it will be that much better for us."

Bowing his head respectfully to Yoshiko, he acknowledged the courage of her act and the difficulty in performing it. She had gained much respect in his eyes. She was what a woman should be. She was samurai. The best of her kind.

He helped Casca drag the bodies farther into the woods and cover them with stones and rubble. It would not be long before someone discovered them, but by then they would be far away. Time was what they needed most, perhaps this would buy them a little more.

Yoshiko joined them as the last of the stones were piled over the dead. She joined Muramasa in saying prayers for the spirits, asking their forgiveness for taking them from this life in order to appease their spirits. It was always wise to do this when time permitted. In violent times such as these, this was done very seldom.

They encountered no more difficulties. Eventually they had to leave the mountain trails and take the more traveled roads leading to Bitchu where they would find, they hoped, the aid that Yoshiko had spoken of.

The temptation to stay at an inn for wayfarers was great but had to be avoided. Instead, they slept under the stars, thankful that the rains had not come.

Several times on their journey, Muramasa had tried to prod Yoshiko into telling him the real purpose of her journey. This was naturally to no avail. She deftly dodged each question and each time turned the game around to him so he was telling her about himself. Then he would forget about his questions for a few minutes until it was too late to pursue them gracefully.

The only one not totally dejected by the descent into the coastal lands was Casca. He kept his attention occupied by observing the people of the islands of the gods. There was a most strange caste system here. Everyone a grade higher had the power of death over those beneath him. One merely had to say the word and the person was immediately killed, or if he was samurai, he had to cut his own belly open in a ritual suicide called *seppuku*. There were safety factors built into the system, though naturally they were heavily weighted in favor of the noble classes. If a man ordered too many deaths, he could possibily offend his lord, who might then command him to commit *seppuku*.

That was only one of their strange customs. The other more important one was the universal adoration of their emperor as the living descendent of the gods. Yet he had no actual power. To deal in earthly matters was to degrade himself. Instead, he had counselors and advisors who took over the common chores of administering his empire.

In reality, the emperor was more a captive than anything else, though several, such as the retired Emperor Go-shirikawa, retired before an untimely death claimed them. As retired emperors, they held great prestige and were free from their lofty godlike positions and could, without loss of face, meddle in human affairs. This combined with the Nihonjin samurai code called *bushido*—the way of the warrior, which exalted noble death above all else—made for those in power a formidable force with which to enforce their will.

Casca had the scandalous thought that just maybe the ones who ran the country and fought over control of the emperor did not have quite the same reverence for their god-king as the common man and samurai did. To them, he was only an instrument by which power could be obtained and the population controlled.

That was what was occurring now. Yoritomo Minamoto, head of the clan by the same name, had once been the power in the land until overthrown by the Taira. Now the clan was coming back. And as the basis by which to rally forces to them, they had the retired Emperor Go-shirikawa who was in their power. Through him, they made the claim that the boy Emperor Antoku was in actuality being held captive by the heretic lords of the Taira. This was reinforced by Go-shirikawa who acknowledged that that was the case and called for a general uprising against the Taira.

To that effect, the country was in a state of civil war with the barons and great landowners choosing sides or straddling the fence while paying lip service until they saw which way the wind would blow. Many of them were disillusioned by the rule of the Taira who kept their family members in all positions of great influence and ignored their allies who helped them in their rise to power.

The Taira were arrogant and cruel. They came from an uncultured tribe who, by good fortune, cunning, and incredible cruelty, rose to power. Now they were even marrying their daughters into the royal line to further secure their claims of control over the emperor.

Other factors included several cults, which were even more confusing to Casca, of so-called warrior monks who did not hesitate to wage war on the samurai or competing cults. They even had occasionally attacked the capital of Heian-Kyo when their wishes or demands were not met by whomever controlled the emperor at that time. These monks were said to be every bit as vicious as samurai without having to deal with the samurai version of morality, which made them very sneaky bastards and very difficult to deal with.

Assassins, warrior monks, religious cults, private armies, warlords and god-kings. This country had it all. Casca wondered if they would ever get together with so many different factors pulling them apart. If they did, they would be hell on wheels and very hard to stop, for their energy and concentration were incredible. Once they decided on something, there was no stopping them short of death.

Trying to put it all into some kind of order made Casca's head swim, so he took the easy way out and just accepted whatever it was until he found out differently. Even though for Casca this was all very confusing. It seemed to make sense to everyone else around him so he didn't ask any embarrassing questions. He didn't even know which questions they might find embarrassing. Therefore, he just kept his mouth shut and listened when Muramasa and Yoshiko spoke of the world as they knew it.

The most he could make out of it was that now was the critical time for the Minamoto clan. If they were ever to reclaim their power, they would have to do it now. There would be no second chance. If they failed, they would be exterminated to the last of their line. This had almost happened once before, but the Taira overlord had fallen in love with a Minamoto woman and permitted her son to live. It was from this act that the Minamoto had resurrected their power and now threatened the Taira.

Though he'd had no say in the matter, it looked as if Casca were aligned with the Minamoto whether he liked it or not. Ever since the first day when Muramasa had found him on the beach, his course had been determined.

Now he would have to go with the sword maker and the strange, beautiful Lady Yoshiko, who could kill with such dispatch, to see what the future held. He had no doubt that it would be extremely violent, for that seemed to be the final argument for everything in this land of shining swords and cherry blossom women. Beauty and death walked hand in hand, touching everything about them equally, at least until the end, when death always reigned supreme. Even then they tried to make that into something of beauty with ritual and ceremony.

This night they found sanctuary beside the gardens of a monastery where saffron-robed monks with shaved, oiled heads tolled huge bronze bells by striking them with tree logs hung from ropes.

Their presence was ignored, but Casca did see that several of the monks carried very workmanlike swords and spears with them. And the monastery had walls which were guarded at night by armed men. He shook his head. Over the years he'd found that when religion takes up arms, the world is in a lot of shit. There should always be a law separating them. He was in the midst of this contemplation when Yoshiko came to stand beside him as he watched the walls.

"Do I disturb your thoughts, *gaijin-san*? If so, I shall retire and leave you to your solitude."

"No, Yoshiko-san, you do not disturb me. I was merely speculating on life."

She moved closer. The scent of jasmine was in her hair, which she had let down to fall nearly to the back of her knees in midnight clouds.

"*Ah so desu.* It is good to think of life. This sad land of mine is filled with too much death."

He thought that strange coming from a whisp of a girl who could drive a chisel-tipped knife into the eye socket of a man, then less than five minutes later cut the throat of her maid.

Sensing his distress, she bowed her head in the moonlight. "I know that you are very disturbed over what happened in the mountains, Casca-san. I shall try to explain as best I can, for it is not easy to understand, even for one such as I who have been raised in these beliefs. So please do me the kindness of listening to me." She paused to await his answer.

When none came she took it for acceptance. It was true that over the last days she had noticed a difference in his attitude toward her, not hostility, but something else, which bothered her. She told herself she needed this *gaijin* with his strong arms to help her reach Kamakura. She could not let him alienate himself from her at this critical stage of their journey.

"Very well then, Casca-san. I do not ask you to feel as I and my kind do. But if you are to survive in these lands, you must know certain things. We are samurai, men and women, and for us there is no greater duty than honor and service to our family and liege lords. Only the emperor is above them, and he is too far away for us to touch, and we will not even attempt to bother him with our petty problems. He is a god; without him, there would be no Sun Rise Empire. He is the weaver's thread that holds the fabric of our culture together. Whether he is truly a god does not matter. He is the symbol of everything for us. He represents all our hopes. Without him, we lose our dreams and the things which make us know we are a special people."

Casca interrupted her a bit tersely. He'd known others who'd claimed to be gods before. As a rule they stunk to the high heavens. "What of the killing, Yoshiko-san?"

"Ah yes, Casca-san. That is the most terrible part. For it is sad to see a life cut down before it can blossom fully into true enlightenment. But in death we find solace. When one loses the fear of death, one is more open and honest with oneself. Fear leaves and the soul is free to find its true karma. And this loss of fear can only be possible when one has devotion to the gods and honor. Without this, the fear of death returns and makes of us a small people in heart and soul. For me to take the life of my maid was, as I said, and I said truly, a most terrible thing. But my duty comes first even before myself. I would not hesitate to take my life as quickly as I did hers. And there is this. She lived long years always in fear of the inevitable. Now her fears are gone. She will come again into this world reborn. I hope as a stronger person, for she was good of heart."

She paused, took a breath, and then sighed, looking at the walls of the ancient monastery looming above them in the night shadows.

"I do hope you understand us better, Casca-san. Duty is that which binds us together. Without it, we would fall apart."

Yoshiko turned from him, gave a graceful bow, and faded back into the darkness leaving him with, "Duty, Casca-san. You will have yours to do also. And you will know it when it comes to you. *Oyasumi nasai*, Casca-san."

CHAPTER ELEVEN

It was the eighth day since they'd landed on Honshu that Yoshiko at last pointed into the distance.

"There is the castle of Kujo Yoshimitsu, a kinsman by marriage. It is here that I pray we will find succor and news."

It was with great relief that they started down the trail leading to the castle, which by any standards was impressive. To Casca's practiced eye, it was well laid out with deep moats on three sides and cliffs on the other. At the top of the walls were parapets and protected positions for archers and arbalesters. When they reached a checkpoint two kilometers from the castle, Casca tensed up as did Muramasa. There were at least a hundred fully armed and armored guards.

Yoshiko calmed them with soothing words. "It is well, these are samurai of my kinsman. Though he pays lip service to Taira, he is his own man and rules this province as his own. The Taira would like very much to destroy him, but he has too many friends and relations among the other great families for them to do so with ease. As long as he does not cause trouble, they are content to look the other way and leave him alone.''

Kicking her animal ahead of them, she commanded, ''Wait. It will be best if I go alone. There are more guards here than when I last came to visit. Perhaps something is amiss. Therefore, I shall go to them first and smooth the passage to my kinsman.''

They did as she said but kept close to their weapons in case things had changed more than she thought. Both felt much better when they saw the samurai guards at the checkpoint bow deeply to her and point to the castle. One of them immediatly took off at a run, obviously carrying word that the Lady Yoshiko no Hirimoto had arrived.

With an imperious wave of her hand, she signaled for Muramasa and Casca to join her. Still playing the part of simple porters, they advanced with heads lowered, careful not to look in the eyes of the curious guards. Though once they were up close, Casca did as usual attract more than one very curious stare.

Yoshiko cast this off with, ''Pay no attention to the ugly one. He is as stupid as he looks, being a great hairy Ainu. However, he is very strong and ofttimes one has need of the service of an ox rather than a nightingale. Especially when intelligence is not required.''

The sentries laughed at the small joke and waved them through with an escort of twenty samurai to take her to her kinsman's portal.

As they neared the castle, Casca saw that it had

been well prepared for attack. The cobbled road they were on was wide enough for ten horsemen. When they passed the checkpoint, he knew they were under observation every step of the way. After leaving the checkpoint, the road began to narrow as it became flanked on two sides by twenty-foot-high walls of sheer, polished rock without handgrips, so that the enemy could not climb them for a counterattack. The road had been cut from the native stone, narrowing to where only two horsemen could ride abreast. The others would be bunched up behind them making it impossible to maneuver. This was the length of about fifty meters, a perfect place to ambush and tie up cavalry on the trail from protected positions above.

After they passed through the small gorge, they entered an area where the brush and trees had been cut back, leaving open ground on both sides of the trail, which Casca felt sure was used by archers and spearmen to attack anyone on the road.

Here was another surprise, though not completely. There before them were at least five hundred men wearing colors he had not seen before. A gold dragon on a white standard rose above their camp. All were very alert. At least half of them stood to with weapons at the ready.

He noticed that Yoshiko was becoming somewhat agitated by the increased pulse rate of the vein in her throat. She said nothing. He and Muramasa began to get ready in the event that trouble was going to start, though they would have no chance against these numbers.

He felt tremendous relief when the samurai officer who was obviously in charge of the detachment came forward to greet Yoshiko. He spoke a few rapid words which Casca couldn't make out, then added twenty more of his men to her escort. They and those of her kinsman, Kujo Yoshimitsu, seemed to get on well enough. There were no signs that Kujo's men resented the presence of the other samurai.

Yoshiko was obviously very excited in spite of her efforts to control herself. Casca wished he knew what was going down, but understood that it would have to wait until they were alone.

The escort of men under the white dragon banner went with them as far as the *mitsuki*, the guardhouse at the castle drawbridge. On either side of the *mitsuki* were two massive corner towers, called *yagura*, which overlooked the road and the drawbridge. Armed men bristled from the towers and the walls. And he knew there were others out of sight in the woods and lowlands around the castle.

There was definitely something going on. The men in the castle were on a war footing, and this close to the castle walls he could see recent improvements had been made for its defense. Sharpened stakes designed to impale either infantry or horses had just been planted. Their tips were still fresh and oozing sap.

Yoshiko was greeted again at the portal leading to the inner gate, this time by a woman. She was most certainly a fine lady of great import. That was clear by her manner and those of the samurai around her.

She and Yoshiko bowed and smiled at each other, making many birdlike chirping sounds as they expressed affection and delight at seeing each other once more.

The woman, who Yoshiko referred to as *obasan*, which Muramasa indicated with some hand signs meant she was closely related to Yoshiko, was richly dressed in many layers of fine crisp silk, each designed to complement the ones beneath. Traces and edges of each layer showed when she moved. Her face was whitened by powder and her teeth stylishly blackened. For a moment Casca thought she had no teeth at all, then he recalled that this was also a custom of the ladies of the Chin. The woman took Yoshiko by the hand and led her away, but not before Yoshiko turned to the guards with Muramasa and Casca.

To the captain of their escort, she said most prettily, "Honored sir, will you see that my servants are given food and shelter? They have been most loyal on a long and difficult journey. I would have them treated well and it would be most kind if you left the animals and the packs on them in their care."

The samurai looked with certain distaste at Casca and Muramasa. But it was not his place to question. The servants should be true and loyal, otherwise they should lose their heads at once. Still, the ways of women were ofttimes hard to understand for a simple warrior.

Yoshiko was led off by the other woman who was saying something about the need for a proper bath and fresh clothes after such a tedious trip. He and Muramasa were taken into a large courtyard. It was from here that he had his first look at the fortifications of a Nihon castle. It was built to last. Huge blocks quarried from native stone were set without the use of mortar. There was no need, just the weight of the stones would hold them in place. There were stables, barracks, cook houses and arms rooms. And most impressive of all, with the exception of Chin, was that it was incredibly clean and kept that way as was evidenced by the numbers of small stoop-shouldered women with whisk brooms. They moved like worker ants around the courtyard removing every piece of dust that fell almost before it touched the stones.

They were turned over to the care of an *ahsi-gari*, the lowest-ranked retainers in a noble household. With obvious distaste, he showed them to simple quarters in the back of the castle where they were given *futomi* to sleep on. Then with a great sniff from an overlarge nose, he told them where they might bathe.

Before they went to clean up they took their packs from their horses and brought them inside their small cubicle for safe keeping. Not that they thought any in this place would steal, for to do so, if caught, was to die. They just did not want any curious eyes to see their weapons and ask questions as to why two simple porters would have such things in their possession.

After luxuriating in a hot bath and changing into

fresh crisp silk robes lent to her by her Aunt Mitsuko, Yoshiko felt almost human. The long ride was over, at least for a time. She had thought her tail-bone would be driven up through her spine, but she could not let the common people with her know of her discomfort or they might have insisted on taking more stops to rest.

Now she was ready to find out what the warriors of the Minamoto were doing here far from their own provinces. Her aunt had avoided her question saying for her to wait until after she had refreshed herself. Then she would be told all. The events leading to Yoshiko's sister's death had long been known to her and there was no time for mourning. She did let Yoshiko know before she bathed that she had heard the sad news, but as samurai women they must put their feelings second to their duty.

Mitsuko came for her after she had sufficient time to prepare herself. At last she was properly gowned and her hair dressed and set with long jewel-tipped pins. It seemed strange to Yoshiko to have the bleached rice powder on her face again and tint on her lips and cheeks. But at least she was once more a lady of quality for all to see and note.

When she answered the tap of a discreet finger on the *shoji,* a sliding door, she knelt with good grace to open it for her aunt.

"*Ah so desu?* Yoshiko-chan. You are very lovely. It is good that the terrible journey did not mar your beauty, for it will be of value to you and your family this day." Holding a finger to her lips, she said,

"Shhh. Ask me nothing now. Just follow me and have faith, for as I promised earlier all will be answered for you in a few more moments. Patience is the spice of fulfillment."

As with all women, her curiosity was incredible, but she had learned as a child when to control it. She glided after her aunt's soft steps until they came to a door that she knew led to the chamber where her kinsman, by marriage to her mother's sister, held audience. Had Yoritomo sent the samurai to aid Kujo in some matter? Or were they here to make certain of his loyalty in the coming battles? She did not know, but four samurai guarded the doors, hands to the hilts of their swords. Two were Kujo's and two were Minamoto's.

With the tension building in her breast, the doors began to slide open ever so slowly until at last she saw what her *obasan*, Mitsuko, had promised was to come true.

Seated in the center of a long low back-lacquered dais, flanked by Kujo on his left and his son, Yeshitsune, on the right, was her master and lord— Yoritomo Minamoto.

CHAPTER TWELVE

It was the hour of the boar and the sun was just beginning to fall behind the mountains when Muramasa and Casca were summoned. It was with reluctance they had to leave their weapons behind, but they knew there was no way they would be permitted to carry them in this household without permission of the master.

Not knowing what to expect, they followed quietly behind the same large-nosed retainer who had shown them to their cubicle. As Casca had suspected, the castle was on war footing. Armed guards were everywhere and they were alert and sharp-looking. They eyed him and Muramasa suspiciously as they passed them on their way to wherever they were going.

When the retainer stopped in front of a *shoji* guarded by both the samurai of Kujo and the samurai of Minamoto, he halted. He hissed under his breath for them to show proper respect and to watch their manners or they would surely lose their heads. Kneeling down in front of the *shoji*, he spoke softly with many bows, though the listener on the other side could not see him. A moment passed before a voice whispered back. He bowed his head to the floor, slid back on his knees, and waited.

The *shoji* slid open, a kneeling samurai attendent bowed and then motioned silently with his hand for them to enter. They did as the retainer had, dropping to their knees they tried to move gracefully into the chamber. They failed miserably as they were not used to these court gymnastics. The attendant who opened the door looked at them with contempt. They were obviously inferior types. But if his master wished to see them, it was not for him to dispute his master's wisdom.

Casca kept his eyes on Muramasa, trying to emulate every movement. Somehow he knew when the sliding screen opened this was something more than a casual introduction to the kinsman of Yoshiko.

Muramasa went in first, bowing his head to the *tatami* mats, not raising his eyes. Casca did the same, slightly behind Muramasa. A voice barked at them hoarsely and they were permitted to raise their heads. It was then that Casca, for the first and last time, laid eyes on Yoritomo Minamoto.

He was by any standards a most impressive specimen. His face was full fleshed with a sharp hooked nose set firmly between heavy eyebrows. His eyes were dark, steady, with no sign of emotion in them. Only stark, clear intelligence gave them any fire. He was wearing armor in the style of *shida-kawa-odoshi*, a breastplate of black-stained steel engraved with the

sign of the dragon and the mantis, accented by white
and blue cords. Over this was a glorious surcoat of
plum satin under a cloak of purest blue silk.

He sat cross-legged on a slightly raised dais behind a long knee-high black table. On either side of
him sat men of importance. One he took to be
related to Yoritomo, though he was younger and
much leaner, more like a falcon where Yoritomo
was an eagle. On the other side sat a samurai noble
with heavy features accented by incredibly thin slits
for eyes so fleshy you barely made them out. Across
his lap lay a sheathed *katana*. Only he was armed.
Casca took this to mean that he was a man whom
Yoritomo trusted and was showing him honor by
permitting him to have his weapons in his presence.

To his left and slightly behind, Yoshiko knelt. Casca
almost lost his breath. He had never seen her in full
dress. She was unbelievable. The women in the street
he had seen in Kyushu were as weeds in a garden of
orchids by comparison. She permitted herself only
the slightest of smiles behind a painted fan, then
lowered her eyes.

Yoritomo motioned for them to come closer.
Muramasa slid ahead three knee lengths, then halted,
placing his head back to the mat once more. Casca
followed suit. Another bark and once more they were
permitted to raise their heads. Casca had the idea
that the retainer who had escorted them had been
absolutely correct. One mistake and their heads would
have rolled on the floor instantly.

Yoritomo spoke again, this time less harshly. The
man with the sword addressed them.

"My niece, Lady Yoshiko, has told us of your service to her and through her to our master. She has told us that you have slain many of the Taira dogs during your journey to us. That is good. There is nothing like the blood of an enemy to know one's friends."

A slight, almost silent hissing halted the conversation. The *shoji* slid open and their packs were brought in by a kneeling samurai who handed them over to the attendant samurai who opened the *shoji*, bowed his head to the floor, and backed out on his knees, never once raising his eyes. There was nothing but silence when Kujo gave the attendant at the *shoji* permission to open the packs. From them everything was removed, clothes and pots and the weapons they had taken from the Taira they had slain and their own weapons. Of the weapons, none attracted any attention but two. The first was that of Sakai no Taira, the sword *Willow Song*.

Yoritomo motioned for the blade to be brought to him. Taking it from its sheath, he admired the workmanship, careful not to touch the bare metal with his flesh. He handed it to his younger brother, Yeshitsune, who examined it closely, then whispered into Yoritomo's ear. Yoritomo nodded in agreement, then Yeshitsune gave it back to the attendant who placed it in front of Muramasa.

Yoritomo nodded his head and spoke to them directly, his voice as always, harsh, demanding, unforgiving to anyone and anything that failed him. "You, *ronin*. I know this weapon. It was the property of Sakai Taira, an old, old acquaintance of mine. How came you by it?''

Muramasa nearly swallowed his tongue, but somehow he found the words.

''I took it from his dead hand, my Lord Yoritomo-sama.'' He used the title of respect when one spoke to a high lord. ''I killed him in single combat and have brought this sword and the others to you, if you will accept such a poor thing from such as we.''

Yoritomo grunted before he spoke.

''It is not such a poor thing this *Willow Song*. It was made by a master sword smith, Sanjo Kokaji. It is a treasure sword worth more than you and your barbarian could earn selling your swords in all your lives, even if you had three of them.''

He looked at the other stack of weapons taken from the dead Taira, then cut his eyes to Yoshiko.

''I would not believe that common *ronin* such as yourself and your barbarian companion could have taken such trophies, except that the Lady Yoshiko has told me of your fighting skills. Therefore, I naturally accept all that she has said of you to be true, for she is a lady of great honor and purity whom I cherish highly. You have earned our gratitude. I accept *Willow Song*.''

With that he clenched his jaws tightly, returning his face to its permanent scowl.

Kujo took over the conversation again.

''Our master feels you have done well in your service to the Lady Yoshiko and to him. He wishes to know what you wish that he may reward you with for your services?''

Muramasa did not hesitate to speak for both of them. Casca was glad of it. He did not want to have any more conversation with the dour and dangerous master of the Minamoto than he had to. The man was a stone killer and his brother, Yeshitsune, didn't look any better.

"Lord Yoritomo-sama, we beg only to be permitted to enter your service for the glory of your name and family. That and nothing more is a greater reward than such as we could hope for."

Yoritomo said nothing. His eye was on the sheathed *Well Drinker*. "Remove the blade from its sheath," he commanded.

Nearly swallowing his tongue, Muramasa did as he was ordered. Taking *Well Drinker* into the flat of both of his palms, he lowered and extended his arms in the direction of Yoritomo. It was a great honor for him to be permitted to bare a weapon in the presence of the master.

Yoritomo did not take the sword into his hands, only looked at it from his dais. He knew great art when he saw it, but there was something about the *katana* that made him keep his hands to himself. Carefully he ran his eyes over it and knew the weapon was perfectly balanced and the steel in the blade as fine as any he had ever seen, better even than *Willow Song*, perhaps even as great as the legendary sword of his ancestor, Yasutsuna, called *Dojo-kiri*, the *Monster-cutter*. But it was now in the hands of the hated Taira who insulted the Minamoto every day that it was in their possession.

Yeshitsune did not have the same qualms as his older half brother. He, too, recognized *Well Drinker* as being something very special, and as some men do for a woman or gold, he lusted after the blade. It was with difficulty he kept the lust from showing. He also felt something in the shining, glowing steel, something that drew him to it.

Lowering his eyelids, Yoritomo carefully reexamined the two men before him. There was something about them, as there was about the sword held in the *ronin's* outstretched hands. He had not come this far without being able to sense things that were unsaid and often unseen. These two would be of value to him, somewhere, sometime. That he was certain of.

"Place your *katana* back into its house for now, Muramasa-san. You will have need of it later. May I ask if it has a name yet?" Yoritomo inquired almost politely.

"Ah yes, thank you, Yoritomo-sama. The blade is called *Well Drinker*." At that, Yoritomo insisted he tell of how the sword came by its name.

Reluctantly, but with pride, Muramasa told of killing the two by the spring of his father after the forging of the blade and of the excellence of the first cut the sword had made.

Yoritomo asked Casca if he had witnessed this act. Casca bowed his head acknowledging that it was so.

Yoshiko coughed delicately behind her painted fan. Yoritomo turned his attention to her.

"You wish to say something, Lady Yoshiko-san?"

Nodding her head prettily, she spoke. "Thank you, my lord. I wish only to add that I have seen the man Muramasa perform such cuts with this *Well Drinker*. It is truly an awesome sword and he is a most accomplished fighter. That is all."

Yoritomo came as close as he ever did to a smile, which was in truth no more than a twisting of the upper lip.

Leaning toward Muramasa, he said, "It seems that once more Lady Yoshiko has come forth to verify what you have done. Very well. You may place yourselves in my service. I give you into the care of my younger brother, Yeshitsune, who I am confident will find more than sufficient work for your *Well Drinker* and your barbarian who I understand is very strong."

Muramasa bowed his head before speaking. As usual, Casca kept quiet. "Yes, Lord, he is very strong, more so than any man I have known before. Though he does lack finesse in the use of the *wazakiri* or *katana*, his strength is such that he simply smashes through his opponents' defenses, then either stabs them to death or sometimes takes their heads in his hands and breaks their necks."

Yoritomo spoke to Kujo in a whisper. Kujo nodded his head and summoned to him the attendant kneeling by the *shoji*. He spoke into his ear and the attendant vanished behind another screen to reappear within three minutes. He had been to the room where the trophies of Kujo's families were kept. In his hand he held a long straight sword more like those from Europe that Casca was familiar with. It was made for two hands and weighed nearly twelve pounds. It would take a very strong man to use one of them for very long in combat.

Yoritomo nodded his head at the samurai attendant who back-scuttled across the floor on his knees to place the large sword in front of Casca.

"Take this then, barbarian, and use it well on my enemies and you shall be well appreciated in this land. Perhaps it will suit your large body and hands more than the *wazakiri* or *katana*. Each to his own. May it bring you good fortune, for this sword has come down through the dark years to us. It is old and has fought more times than the trees have blossoms. Use it well with honor and prosper."

With that, the audience was at an end. They crawled backwards out of the presence of the lord of the Minamoto.

This time Yoshiko smiled openly, pleased that her words had been able to help her companions of the road. It was the least she could do and perhaps the most. Now as Yoritomo had commanded, he would talk to her alone without any others being in attendance.

CHAPTER THIRTEEN

Yoshiko and Yoritomo were left alone in the open room. Even the attendant by the *shoji* had been dismissed. Yoritomo indicated for Yoshiko to come and sit by him while he poured tea for both of them. It was a sign of singular honor for him to do so. Waiting until each had taken several courteous sips of the steaming brew, Yoritomo set his eggshell-thin porcelain cup down on the table.

"My child, I am very pleased with you. You have lived up to my every expectation. Now I am going to ask something of you that will be very difficult. I would not make this request of you if I did not consider it to be of the greatest import. Your acceptance will save many thousands of lives and most probably guarantee our success, especially now that you have given me the Kwanto."

Yoshiko bowed her head, holding her teacup between long graceful fingers.

"My life is yours, my lord," she responded quite simply and honestly.

"I know, my child, and that is what I am asking you for. Your life."

Her heart caught in her breast. It was a struggle to control the tremor in her voice as she repeated, "My life is yours, my lord. What must I do?"

Yoritomo wanted to reach out and touch her but could not. His responsibilities were too great to let the life of one woman interfere. And it was true. She could by her death save the lives of thousands of his men who would be needed for the final battle.

He bowed as deeply as he could to show his respect for her. "I promise you, Yoshiko-chan, that your gift will do as much, if not more than an army of ten thousand men. With your gift I will have all I need. Now I have not only the retired Emperor Go-shirikawa but the brother of Antoku, Gotoba, under my protection. Our armies have taken all the provinces of the north, and even the Yamabushi mountain warriors have rallied to me as well as most of the warrior monks. Yours is the last offering I need to make everything we have worked for for so many years come to pass. I thank you, Yoshiko-chan." Again he used the expression of great fondess and affection.

"Now this," he continued, returning to his more familiar stern and cold visage, "is the way in which it shall be done. Listen closely, my child . . ."

They talked long into the night before Yoshiko was permitted to leave him and retire to her chambers, exhausted emotionally and physically. She at last cried herself to sleep. At times it was very hard to be samurai, but she would not fail her duty and her promise to her lord, though there were many pleasant things left to experience in this life. Muramasa and Casca passed through her thoughts and she blushed delicately.

In the morning when the sun rose at the hour of the dragon, Muramasa and Casca were summoned to Yeshitsune who waited for them in the courtyard.

"You have been given to me to deal with. Get your things ready to travel. Your horses are being prepared. We ride for the north and battle."

To Casca he pointedly said, "Do not fail me at anything, barbarian. You remind me too much of the hairy Ainu, whom I detest. I suggest you stay close to your companion, Muramasa-san, whom I recognize as being a great artist. You may also know that my brother has given me full power to reward or punish you in his name. Whatever I decree will be the same as if from his own lips."

They wished to say farewell to Yoshiko but this was not permitted.

"Do not trouble me with your petty problems. I have a war to finish and you are now part of that war to the end, to victory or death, possibly both. See yourselves to your animals and be ready to ride in ten minutes!"

They had no choice. Returning quickly to their chamber, they gathered their belongings together and hurried back to where their horses had already been brought into the courtyard and were waiting for them. Not knowing just where to fit in, they found a gap between the two companies of cavalry that would accompany Yeshitsune. The rest of the Minamoto samurai would remain behind with Yeshitsune's brother to serve as his escort.

Casca had the feeling that he might not ever lay eyes on Yoshiko again. A terrible and great sadness came over him. He had liked her very much, might possibly even have been a bit in love with her. Now he felt he would never know. A look at Muramasa, whose eye he caught, and he knew the *ronin* felt the same way. They nodded to each other as if to say, karma, and rode after Yeshitsune to enter the last stages of the war against the Taira.

For the next weeks they marched and fought pitched battle after battle, Yeshitsune always taking the lead. He was quick and better than most of his peers in the use of tactics and movement.

While Yeshitsune was in the field his brother, Yoritomo, was taking care of the final details. Conducting few actions himself, his main interest was the alignment of the families of power and the alienation of them from the Taira. He moved into the Kwanto. The passes were open to him and closed to the Taira.

Yeshitsune had earlier advanced his army to where it threatened the northern flank of Heian-Kyo, forcing the Taira to respond with a movement of large numbers of their forces. That was when Yoritomo broke through to take the imperial city. He was too late to take the boy Emperor Antoku into his protection but all else fell to him. The Taira were split and driven south. This victory he dedicated publicly to Yoshiko, for without her it might not have been.

It was a sad thing she had to do and a magnificent one. His torturers found out the rest of the story from prisoners before their heads joined the piles set in front of the gates of Heian-Kyo. There were Taira heads there by the thousands.

Yoshiko had been sent with a written message from Yoritomo to certain nobles, thanking them for their support and promise of aid in the revolt against the Taira. To each of the nobles he promised the lands and estates of the enemy when victory was theirs. This was written in a code to which he knew the Taira already had the key. Subterfuge was Yoritomo's strongest point, the ability to use the paranoia that exists within the breast of power.

He would give the Taira something they could not refuse to believe. Lady Yoshiko was that something. As was planned, she and her escort were intercepted by the samurai of Taira who guarded and patrolled the roads he knew she must take after visiting three of the names on the letters of thank you. Her escort fought to the death and she was taken prisoner.

Because of her rank, she was brought before Koremori Taira, the Prime Minister of Antoku. There, as the story was related to him, Lady Yoshiko stood up to every threat, refusing to answer any questions. Then, when Koremori showed her the letters with the code broken, she had broken into tears and begged him to permit her to wipe out the disgrace of failure.

Yoritomo knew Koremori well and the one thing he liked more than power was death. He granted her wish.

Yoshiko was permitted to prepare herself with the aid of Minamoto women who had been held as hostages for their men's good behavior. She had dressed all in white, the color of mourning, accented with red silk undergarmets to signify her ready acceptance of her fate. The women dressed her hair, tying it up high to bare her long graceful neck. Then with great grace and style she had taken the dagger given to her by one of her attendants, and with steady hands and clear eyes she cut the great vein in the neck in the rite called *kwaiken*. She then lay her head in a cushioned wicker basket so that her blood would not stain her clothes and she died.

This was the final proof that Koremori needed to prove the letters were true. The death of Yoshiko had given him that. She could not live with her disgrace and failure. That he understood.

Immediately he sent troops to attack the new rebels, taking many thousands of men away from the defense of the city. He had to do it or all would have been lost if the rebels had time to join their forces with Yoritomo.

The letters were false. All that he accomplished was to throw the names on the letters into the arms of the Minamoto rebels, causing him to split his forces at a critical time of Yoritomo's choosing. And when the passes from the Kwanto were opened to Yoritomo, he did not have enough men to defend against him.

Now Koremori was involved with a series of running battles along the southern coasts, taking Antoku with him. His plans, which Yoritomo already knew from his spies in Koremori's camp, were made. They would have their next battle at a place of his choosing.

He was already gathering ships and forcing thousands of peasants into his ranks to replenish those fallen in combat. It was a pity there was no time to train most of them properly, but their deaths would still aid his cause. He would throw the inexperienced peasants into the front ranks to tire out the sword arms of the Minamoto, then he would send in his fresh, strong, battle-tested and proven samurai against them. Even outnumbered, that should give him an equal chance for victory. And with his fleet to maneuver, he would be able to land troops behind the supply lines of the Minamoto, reducing their ability to stay in the field.

All he needed was this one victory, then he would begin to roll up the enemy, advancing back to the north and Heian-Kyo. He was not through yet! There were still many lords who would lose their lives and lands if they did not come to his aid. They had served him too long. Yoritomo was certain to take vengeance against them if he was victorious.

All this and more Yoritomo knew and he was quite content. To those who had supported the Taira, he promised on the most sacred vows that he would take no vengeance. They would put all past grievances behind them and work together for a new day. This he swore by Gentle Bhudda and by the ancient and terrible gods of war. To this he signed his family's honor to the end of time.

But if they did not join him, then it would also be true that they would die and lose their rank and lands forever. Their children would be sold into slavery and their women taken as whores for his soldiers to play with. To this he also swore the same great oaths. He was believed. Few came to the Taira ranks.

Koremori was alone in the south. There would be just this one last battle, then all would be done and the Minamoto would reclaim their rightful place.

If there was a sadness to the sacrifice of Yoshiko, there was also great joy. For she would be forever honored and remembered. Her story would become legend to live beside the great heros of antiquity. There would be a thousand plays and songs written of her once he told the truth about her courage and how she saved thousands of Minamoto warriors from death.

Hers was a most lonely death, but then does not each die alone even when surrounded by thousands? Is not each death singular, something that can never be truly shared or felt by another?

For the first time in his memory, he shed a single tear. He would, in her memory, write a poem.

CHAPTER FOURTEEN

During the battles for the northern approaches, Yeshitsune's men came into fierce battle with a clan of warrior monks of the Sohei cult. Only after fierce resistance was the monastery, which was really a fort, captured, but only after the loss of men at a three-to-one ratio in favor of the monks. Casca was glad there weren't more of them or it might have gone very badly. As it was, his regiment of six hundred men had to stop for several days to rest and bind their wounds.

He and Muramasa put their rest time to good use, taking advantage of the hot springs that lay below the monastery in a green glen. Here the waters bubbled, even during the coldest winters, keeping the valley perpetually green and fresh. Birds sang and flowers bloomed in profusion.

Casca thought he would have liked for Yoshiko to have been there with them. She would have seen it with different eyes and explained it to him. As it was the waters were warm and soothing to weary, strained muscles.

Muramasa sat on a submerged boulder covered with soft green water grass, letting the heat soak deep into his flesh, luxuriating in the warmth.

Eyeing Casca across the pond, he wondered again about the many scars on his body. They had been together now for some months and he still knew little of the *gaijin* and his past or even how he came to be cast upon the shores of Kyushu. Closing his eyes, he submerged his head for a moment under the hot steaming waters, then rose again. Shaking the water from his face and hair as a dog would whip droplets from its pelt, he returned to his idle speculation of Casca. He looked at the new scar among the many others. He had seen that one take place not two days ago.

He and Casca, with a detachment, had been attacking the south walls of the monastery when a light throwing lance had struck the *gaijin* in the lower abdomen. He had seen the head of the lance penetrate to a depth of at least ten inches. The *gaijin* had pulled it out and continued the battle, though he was obviously in much pain and his huge antique battle sword did great damage among the warrior monks of the Sohei. It was a wound, which if not fatal, should certainly have incapacitated him for several weeks. He did lie down after the fight for a full night and now here he was, as good as new, and the wound was closed, looking as if it were already several years old.

This was not the only time he had seen such things happen to his strange friend. More and more he thought that perhaps Casca and his sword *Well Drinker* were somehow connected. Both had awesome powers.

Breast-stroking, Casca swam over to Muramasa and sat down beside him in the warm waters.

"What do you think of the things Yeshitsune told us about Yoshiko?" He blurted this out most unexpectedly.

Yeshitsune had told them before they went into action against the monks that Yoshiko had died by her own hand and she had died nobly. That was all, and this he gave out only reluctantly. Casca was certain that his brother, Yoritomo, had ordered him to tell them of her death or they might not have known for months.

Muramasa lowered his face into the water giving him an opportunity to gather his thoughts. Pulling his head back up, dripping, he shook the warmness from his face. "I do not know, Casca-san. She was a most exceptional woman. I am sure that she did die well, that is all I can tell. I feel as if we have both lost one who would have been a great friend to us forever. I miss her very much. Perhaps someday we will know the entire story but if not, her memory is alive in us and will live as long as we do."

Casca nodded his head in agreement. Yes, if that was so, then Yoshiko-chan would indeed live a very long time. After all the great lords of the Sun Rise Empire had long been turned to dust and their swords rusted away, she would still live in his memory. Of that he was also certain, for she had indeed been a most exceptional woman.

There was a long awkward silence then. At last Muramasa, as Casca had earlier, blurted out, "Casca-san, if it would not offend you, would you tell me something true about yourself?"

Casca had seen this coming for some time, since the first arrow had sunk into his left shoulder at the battle of Hase Kannon outside of Kamakura, where the shrine of Kannon, the Goddess of Mercy, watched over eight thousand men as they killed each other with swords, axes, hatchets and arrows. She must have cried great tears of sorrow that day for the blood that was shed by her shrine to mercy and gentleness.

He did have a chance to get one quick look inside at the statue of the goddess. It stood twenty-seven feet high and was carved out of one solid piece of a camphor log. Muramasa had told him the statue of the goddess was around five hundred years old. At any rate it was there that Muramasa had pulled the barbed head from Casca's shoulder. Then as he was cleaning the wound, Muramasa saw it close and become a scar within minutes. It hadn't been very deep, though it did hurt a bit. He'd had much worse. The expression on Muramasa's face when he saw the wound close was like the shutting of an open door. He slammed down everything inside him. It was the same as if he'd seen nothing. He just put his lint and bandages away and walked off saying nothing about it.

He knew it was only a matter of time before Muramasa got around to asking him about his condition. Now that time was here and he wasn't sure what he was going to say. Muramasa was not a fool. He did believe in spirits, had many mystical things that touched him, especially since *Well Drinker* had come into his life. But he was no fool and Casca couldn't treat him like one. He owed the stern little man with the insane sword that much.

That was one conclusion he'd come to. The sword, and not Muramasa, was mad. He wished he'd get rid of it before it turned on him.

"Of course, Muramasa-san. You may ask me anything, but please understand that what I say may not mean exactly the same to you as it does to me. However, I must use your frame of reference."

"*Hai*, Casca-san. I know that we come from very different cultures and do not always see or even feel things in the same manner. But we are men. I mean I am, but are . . ." He left the question unfinished, giving Casca time to back away from it if he chose to.

Casca began his tale, taking Muramasa back through the long centuries past. He told him of his odyssey through time and how he had come to be cursed at Golgotha when he'd driven his lance into the side of the man from Galilee. It had taken him hours and the night was nearly on them. Only the warmth of the hot pool kept the chill away as he finished his story.

Muramasa had sat silent through the tale, at times nodding his head as he understood a fine point, other times shaking it in wonder, even in horror at the road Casca had to take. When it was done, he knew Casca had told him the truth. The evidence had been seen by his eyes more than once. There was magic in the world. Witness *Well Drinker*.

He had made no comment about the tale told by Casca. There was little he could say. He did know that he had to go with the *gaijin* to wherever their road would take them, but it was a heavy burden to carry with him, not only a cursed sword but also a cursed man. He had so many questions to ask. Perhaps one day when the time was right he and the long-nosed one would sit down and he would ask the things that were rushing into his mind. But not now. Now they had battles yet to fight and he was not yet samurai.

CHAPTER FIFTEEN

From the hillside overlooking the Isthmus of Shigimitsu, it was a magnificent spectacle. The samurai were nothing if not incredibly colorful. There were colorful banners and flags, tunics and loose *hakama* trousers of a hundred shades of plum and scarlet, and emerald and gold rippled through the ranks of both sides.

At sea the awkward junk-style vessels wallowed slowly toward each other. The Taira ships inside the narrows of the straits were trying to act as a blocking force but something was going wrong. They were having a hard time maneuvering and the winds were not with them. Perhaps the tides and the winds were against them. The Minamoto were outside moving in, trying to catch the wind and close with the Taira.

They had gone almost full circle, returning to where they had first made their crossing from Kyushu to Honshu. Here in these narrow straits the final chapter was to be written in oceans of blood. Casca was not and had never been a good sailor, though the gods knew he had spent enough time on ships of one kind or another.

From what he could see, his first impressions seemed to be correct. The currents and tides were obviously forcing the Taira ships in close to the shore where they were in danger of breaking up on submerged rocks and reefs or being beached in an area held by the Minamoto forces. Shading his eyes, Casca thought he could make out the ship that bore the boy Emperor Antoku Tenno. The Taira obviously felt he was safer on one of the ships than on land. The ship was in the rear of the fleet surrounded by three other larger war vessels filled with samurai, most of whom would have rather been on the land than on the sea, for the Japanese were not great sailors and few, if any, knew the art of swimming. Any who went into the water would die save those few who the gods would smile upon, or had taken the time to learn to swim.

From where Casca stood, the smell of death was strong. Below he could see thousands of crumpled butterflies lying on carpets of red, the dead of Dan-No-Ura. Both sides had taken heavy losses. Casca had great respect for the courage of the samurai but little for the tactics they employed. Direct confrontation was the method normally favored by both sides. As a rule their generals knew little of the fine art of maneuvering and terrain. But their personal courage was incredible.

His own robes were stiff and sticky with blood. He had fought well this day but Muramasa had been

a man possessed. He and that damned cursed sword
of his. The number of heads he had taken this day
was incredible and it seemed as if nothing could
touch him. *Well Drinker* had killed and blocked all
killing blows made at him. Now they were entering
the final stage of the battle.

The Taira forces were doomed and Casca knew
that very few would live to see Ameratsu on the
morrow. Whoever lost died. That was the rule and it
seemed as if the samurai warriors did not wish it any
other way. There was only victory or death. And
death came either by the enemy's hand or by your
own. To Casca it was a stupid way to do business.
But death to these small fierce butterflies was less
important than their own illusions of the value of
their personal honor. Or was it an illusion? Shiu
Lao-tze had said to him long before, "If you believe
in anything strong enough, is it not true? Perhaps
not for anyone else, for they are not you." And
Casca had seen dreams and fantasies kill before,
dreams of power, gold, vengeance. They all began
as illusions.

Turning his head to the left slightly, he was able
to see Yeshitsune and his staff observing the course
of the battle. Their faces were like rocks, the corners
of their mouths downcast in seemingly perpetual
scowls of dissatisfaction, but he knew they were
well satisfied. They were winning and with the win
came new glory and power for all who served the
white banner of the Minamoto. Even better, the

hated Taira usurpers would be exterminated. Never again would they rise to challenge them for power.

Yeshitsune raised his war fan in a simple off-handed gesture and the sounds began again. From the flanks the *jin-dai-ko* began to beat a drum roll as the drummers received their signals from their officers. Over the din of the thundering basso of the war drums, hitting the high notes in this macabre concert, *hora-gai*, ram horns, started shrilling and the teaming forces of the Taira and Minamoto faced off. The Taira were half encircled on the beach and in such a bad position, they could not use their remaining cavalry to much effect as they had no room to maneuver between the rice paddies on their left flank and the rocky ridges of the coastline on their right.

On their front and both flanks the Minamoto awaited the order to begin the attack. The ships of the Taira were beginning to turn into the shore. Seeing they would have no chance in open battle at sea, the commander had decided that they would take their chances on land rather than face a watery ignoble death at sea. Clumsily they began to tack to the landward. Perhaps if their forces were added to those already facing the armies of the Minamoto, they might have the strength to force the day.

Casca briefly saw the ship he thought bore Emperor Antoku try to come about, then he had to turn his attention back to the fight beginning in front of him. He and Muramasa were assigned to a group of Yeshitsune's own Honyei honor guards. It was they who would have the honor of splitting the Taira forces on the beach into two sections by which they could then be butchered with greater facility.

He and Muramasa were the only ones with blood on their weapons and clothes. The rest of Yeshitsune's personal guards eyed them with obvious envy and even resentment that they had been held back from the battle. He and Muramasa had been brought to Yeshitsune at the end of the last engagement. He had been observing them in action and now he was going to honor them by permitting them to go into the most dangerous part of the battle. They would take the point of his two thousand personal guards and charge straight into the amassed Taira ranks, not stopping until they reached the beach. Once there, they would then hold against attacks from both sides until the remainder of the Minamoto forces engaged and destroyed the Taira who would then be on both of their flanks.

Muramasa was overwhelmed by the honor. Casca was a bit more pragmatic. They were very likely to get their asses cut up badly. Well, he had been told before that he had no true sense of honor. They were right. This was stupid. He was, however, the only one here this day to think so. The samurai of the guards were ecstatic at the honor. Their bodies fairly trembled with expectation.

On the beach the Taira prepared themselves, each man knowing this was most probably his final hour on this earth. They were ready to make their last moments memorable and honorable ones. Each hoped to be remembered with honor by his enemies this day, for there would surely be no friends left alive to speak of it.

Yeshitsune spoke softly into the ear of one of his aides, a portly man who seemed to make up for his lack of physique by scowling more fiercely than anyone else save his master, which of course would have been very bad manners. Bobbing his head and bowing away from the commander, he rushed over to Muramasa. He held his *katana*, which he had never drawn in battle, as he waddled as fast as he could on bent legs. Casca could overhear him as he hissed at Muramasa.

"You have been given a great honor this day. Do not shame our master. He has given you the great distinction of being the first to cast the challenge to the Taira usurpers."

Casca could feel the pride swell up in Muramasa even as he bowed deeply, then fell to his knees facing Yeshitsune and touched his head three times against the earth. Rising, he whispered in the aide's ear, who looked a bit perplexed. Then the aide bobbed his head and raced back to Yeshitsune. Dropping to his knees, he spoke under his breath with much bowing, then waited a moment until Yeshitsune responded, which he did after looking once with blank eyes in his and Muramasa's direction. Casca had a very strong feeling that something was not going his way at all.

Yeshitsune barked a command and the aide scuttled crablike back to Muramasa and whispered in his ear, then left to resume his place at his master's side.

Muramasa came to Casca, his faced flushed, chest swelled, his grip on the haft of *Well Drinker* so tight the knuckles threatened to break through the tough pads of skin surrounding them.

Affecting the same stern countenance of the samurai, Muramasa barked and hissed at Casca who had trouble understanding him when he was like this.

"Ah, long nose. You have no idea of the honor that I have asked for you this day. It will be glorious and you shall share in everything."

Casca was suddenly very reluctant to ask what the "honor" was and what "everything" consisted of. Then he had the very uneasy feeling that Muramasa was going to tell him something he would rather not hear. Therefore, he said nothing, hoping in vain that perhaps Muramasa would just forget what it was he had to say and go away.

"Ah yes, long nose. I have asked for and have been given permission for you to cast the first challenges with me. Think of it! Alone we shall face the best the Taira dogs have to offer and gain the great honor of serving our master, the Minamoto. Is it not a great service I have done for you this day?"

There was no gracious way to tell Muramasa to go fuck off, so instead he took the coward's way out.

"*Hai, honto*, Muramasa-san. It is a great honor you have done this unworthy long-nosed barbarian. I am forever in your debt for the great and kind consideration you have shown this unfortunate and unworthy person this day.''

Muramasa returned Casca's bow, well satisfied. It seemed as if at last the barbarian was learning some proper manners.

Casca's sarcasm fell on deaf ears. He was stuck with the situation. Adjusting his *obi*, he pulled his sword loose from the scabbard as the *jin-dai-ko* signaled for the guards of Yeshitsune to advance to the beach. Being the honored ones, he and Muramasa took the lead.

There were many jealous and envious glances at them from other samurai. That these common *ronin* should be so placed in front of them was almost too much to bear. Several thought to perform the act of *kanshi*, a ritual suicide of protest at their treatment, by which their master would know their deep and most sincere feelings of shame at the dishonor he had done them. That was they would commit suicide if they lived through the rest of the day. However, until they did, their lives were their master's and if he so commanded, then it was to be done. It would be unseemly to make the protest before the fact.

From the hill, Muramasa led the band of bodyguards past the cheering battalions who opened ranks to permit them to pass through. Overhead a number of vultures had gathered, circling the battlefield. They were nearly invisible among smaller black forms that flitted and swooped as they, too, waited patiently for their feast for the day. Ravens by the thousands had come from near and far. Many had crossed the straits from Kyushu to be in at the end of the day's eye-plucking, a favored delicacy among their kind.

Waves of passion rode over the men as they marched to the sea. Muramasa stepped off in long certain strides, eyes straight ahead, acknowledging nothing. This was his moment. Ahead of him lay his future, death or honor. This was his last chance to achieve his life's ambition, and if it could not be reached, then it was best that he die this day.

Leaking net bags were raised up from the soldiers around them, bags Casca knew were for containing the heads of the dead enemy. There were *kubibukuro*, bags for the common dead, and *kubi-oki*, buckets with spikes in the bottom for the heads of noble enemies that would be presented later to Yeshitsune and then to his brother. The heads in the buckets were the important ones, for they would prove that the last of the line of the Taira had been exterminated.

CHAPTER SIXTEEN

As they passed through the legions of the Minamoto, Casca noticed that the cheers they were hearing were somewhat staggered. He and Muramasa received their loudest acclaim when they passed the ranks of the common soldiers, who it appeared took part of the honor being shown Muramasa and Casca unto themselves. The samurai cheered of course, but only for the other samurai of their own class of which he and Muramasa were not members.

The sun had passed its zenith. Heat waves rose and wavered over the dead, taking the heavy cloying smell of blood up to the heavens.

Casca estimated that so far this day over fourteen thousand had died and perhaps that many more would die before the sun fell. The stench of massive death was incredible. The smell of one dead man was bad enough but when it was multiplied ten thousand fold, it was almost overwhelming. But these stalwarts of the Sacred Islands of the Gods didn't seem to notice it at all. They wanted more. Casca had fought for or against a hundred armies—Mongols,

Huns, Romans, Syrians, Visigoths and Persians. None seemed to have the same sophisticated lust for slaughter and death that these men did.

Passing the last rank of pike men and, behind them, three lines of archers, they reached the clearing between their forces and those of the Taira. A space of about three hundred meters lay open in front of them. Across it was the last of the Taira armies that would face the might of the Minamoto. Behind them Casca could see the square sails of their ships coming closer to shore. If they were to win and take minimal losses, they should do it quickly before the Taira ships had a chance to beach and add that strength to their ground forces.

Muramasa halted a moment to view the opposing side. He postured, for this was his day and the eyes of the entire army were locked on him. Looking out the corner of his eye to check on Casca, he moved forward, strutting fiercely. He had the natural-born instincts of an actor and this was to be his greatest stage performance.

Moving out to the center of the cleared area, which was not all that clear as several hundred bodies lay scattered about on it, he halted, pointed *Well Drinker* at the Taira warriors and called out to them.

"I am Jinto Muramasa, son of Kitao the sword maker and killer of Taira scum. I have this day taken fourteen of your warriors' heads, all samurai, and will take twice that number before the last of you die. Is there one who will come to face me? If not, then send two, for my sword has appetite enough for all of you!''

From the Taira came an angry murmur at the insult of a commoner being sent to make challenges reserved for samurai. Arching out of their ranks came a flying shaft set free by a young samurai who did not deem the *ronin* to be worthy of honorable individual combat. The shaft sped straight for Muramasa's chest, then in the flicker of an eye *Well Drinker* moved, slicing the arrow into two, dropping it, useless, to the bloody earth. From the Taira came a spontaneous sigh of admiration. The *ronin* had talent. He was not samurai but he was good. Whoever killed him would be remembered this day if he had indeed taken fourteen heads. There was much sad shaking of heads among the Taira nobles, for their honor would not permit them to accept a challenge from a commoner.

Muramasa stamped his feet in frustration, crying out for them to send three if two would not come and meet him. He was being rejected. The pain of the insult was incredible. Casca just stood by ready to do whatever he had to.

What came next was totally unexpected. A murmur began behind them that grew into a resounding roar: *''Banzai, banzai!''* Then absolute silence. Glancing over his shoulder, Casca saw that Yeshitsune had stepped to the edge of the clearing, hands on the hilts of his swords, feet wide spread. Behind him was his standard bearer with the white pennant with the dragon emblazoned in gold thread. The Taira had no doubt as to who he was.

"I am Yeshitsune no Minamoto. I see that the Taira do not wish to wage single combat with even a common supporter of the Minamoto. Therefore, I declare for all to hear and take note that from this moment onward, in recognition of the services they have given, the man Jinto Muramasa and his companion the *gaijin*, Casca-san, together with their heirs, are forever to be known and respected as true and honorable men. THEY ARE *SAMURAI*!''

Muramasa nearly fainted. Casca frowned. He had hoped for just a moment that because of their low rank they would not have to fight against the Taira champions. No such luck.

From the Taira a voice boomed to answer Yeshitsune. Casca saw a large heavy-boned man in rich armor of the *o-yori* style, but made for war instead of the court, step out of the ranks.

"Thank you for resolving our difficulty, Yeshitsune-san. It is indeed seldom the Minamoto do us such a service. Now that the dogs you have sent are samurai, it is permissible to kill them with no loss of honor. Such an event I always enjoy when they are the scum who lick the boots of the Minamoto.''

From his scabbard he drew a beautiful blade of watered steel.

"I am Tomomori no Taira, brother to Shigimori and son of Kiyomori. I carry the great sword of Yasutsuna, *Dojo-kiri*, the *Monster-cutter*, which was used by your own ancestor Minamoto no Yoshimitsu and taken from your family by mine when we kicked you out of Heian-Kyo and whipped you back to your kennels where you belong. Come and take your ancestor's sword back if you can!''

Behind him came one other who begged permission of Tomomori to kill the *gaijin*. The permission was granted. The two stepped forth on the field. Swords bared, they moved with the confidence of men already victorious. As they neared they separated, each moving to his man.

Casca's opponent was a youngster of, he guessed, about seventeen. His face was as smooth as a baby's bottom and quite handsome with bright clear brown eyes. He had a graceful manner to his walk. If Casca had been able to look closer, he would have seen the robes of silk over his armor had been carefully re-sewn many times. He was a poor boy from a noble family who hoped the war would bring him great rewards. Now all he had to hope for was a valiant death.

Casca moved, setting himself. He knew he was not as fast as these samurai but he had greater strength. The trick was to pick the time to use it.

He had no time to keep an eye on Muramasa. His youthful opponent moved immediately to the attack. His blade work was fast, as Casca had thought it would be, but his technique was not as good as his. Still it took nearly all his talents to keep the young-ster's enthusiastic attacks from breaking through his guard. If there had been any way to avoid it, he would have. But there was no choice. The youngster was a dead man. If not now, then within a few hours he would be. The young man made a sideways slice that Casca blocked, then stepped in close, his sword barring the other's blade, freezing it in position. The young man's face was a study in complete concentration and strain as he tried to break contact, but Casca kept the pressure on, forcing him back one then two steps, giving the young man time to set himself after each shove. Then on the third shove, as the youngster once more tried to set himself, instead of shoving again, Casca stepped back. Unexpected, the sudden release of force jerked the young man forward half a step as he tried to regain his balance. As he did, Cascas's sword quickly plunged in and then back out of his throat. A quick kill. Not following the popular custom of hacking off heads, he turned to see how Muramasa was faring with his opponent, as no one else had come on to the field to challenge him.

Tomomori had come as the *kaze*, the wind. His years had not slowed his arm. *Dojo-kiri*, the legendary *Monster-cutter*, met the *Well Drinker*. When they touched and struck each other, it was as if the bells from the temples of Mount Hiei rang out.

Muramasa met every cut, every thrust, letting *Well Drinker* lead him. No, he did not 'let' *Well Drinker* lead him. He had no choice. The sword took him. His mind was somewhere else observing the fight. Life or death, neither was important, only the dancing, shining *katana* that rang with such beauty with the legendary *wazakiri* of Tomomori. Only in that was there true beauty and meaning. Only in the steel was there any value in life and *Well Drinker*, when it danced, was more than his own soul.

He almost felt *mono no*, a deep pathos, a sweet sadness, which somehow fulfilled him. This was good! It was the way—to not think, to let the sword be the master and take him where it wished. He wanted to weep from pure crystal joy.

Tomomori felt a great weight on his chest, a crushing, heavy weight. His arm grew numb from the repeated counters of the *ronin*. And he was *ronin*, no matter what the bastard Yeshitsune had declared. But where did this common piece of clay find such skill? And look at his face. It was totally unconcerned. No strain, no effort to indicate that they had been fighting for five minutes. Tomomori had known from the first few contacts that he was going to die. But by the gentle Bhudda, he wanted to take this one with him. Stepping back, he lowered his sword point to his knees, gathering his strength for another rush when Muramasa also stepped back, placed *Well Drinker* in its sheath, and turned his back on Tomomori.

From the observers on both sides came a gasp of surprise and awe as Muramasa turned slowly and deliberately away from Tomomori, his *Well Drinker* sheathed.

Tomomori thought his heart was going to burst from its cage. How could he? How could this one turn his back on him? He was Tomomori, lord of three provinces, slayer of more than fifty valiant warriors. How could this piece of offal perform such an act?

With a cry of rage he raised his sword. He would make the *ronin* turn and face him. All slowed down to a time sense that moved as tree sap in the early days of spring. All saw Tomomori leap into the air, *Dojo-kiri* high above his head, Tomomori's arms coming down for the powerful stroke that would split Muramasa into two parts from shoulder to hip. And still Muramasa seemed to ignore the warning cry Tomomori had given.

Dojo-kiri was moving, it seemed, with incredible slowness, though all knew it was traveling faster than the eye could truly see. Then Muramasa moved his body, dropping, knees bending him low to the ground, but his upper body erect as if he were still standing. *Well Drinker* came out of its house using the whipping, turning motion of Muramasa's body and arms. *Well Drinker* and Muramasa began to rise up as they turned to meet Tomomori and *Dojo-kiri* for the last time.

Well Drinker rose higher still. From all sides gasps of awe and wonder came forth spontaneously. Muramasa was making the *iai* cut. *Well Drinker* reversed the slice being made by *Dojo-kiri*.

Entering Tomomori's body at his right hip, *Well Drinker* reached deep, the tip extending six inches behind Tomomori's back. It slid with apparent ease through the armor, flesh and bones, moving up at an angle of thirty degrees until *Well Drinker* broke free of Tomomori's body at the junction of his right shoulder, leaving him in a spray of scarlet as the blood burst forth from severed arteries.

Dojo-kiri never completed its final move. Tomomori dropped to the earth, intestines steaming out of his body cavity, eyes open, his mouth trying to cast one last curse at the demon warrior with the cursed sword. He had heard of *Well Drinker* and its evil. Now as he died he knew it was true. He had felt something when the blade passed through his body. It had been a foretaste of hell.

He died. But just before his eyes glazed over, he saw Muramasa bend over and take *Dojo-kiri* from his own hand, then toss his useless arm away like so much trash.

CHAPTER SEVENTEEN

When Tomomori fell, a groan ran through the ranks of the Taira. Another flashing sweep of *Well Drinker* and his head was held aloft by his samurai topknot. Sheathing *Well Drinker*, Muramasa took up the *wazakiri* sword *Dojo-kiri* and marched to Yeshitsune. Kneeling in front of him, he bowed his head holding his arms outstretched, each hand bearing a gift. In one hand was *Dojo-kiri* and in the other, Tomomori's head.

"Lord, it is my most humble honor that one as unworthy as I should be permitted to return to you the sword of your honorable ancestor."

Yeshitsune took the sword from Muramasa's hand, touched the weapon with a carefully tended nail, bowed over the legendary sword, and handed it with reverence to an attendant. "Take this to my brother, Yoritomo, as a token of my affection. He is the leader of the clan. The sword must be returned to his care. Should anything happen to the sword, you are ordered to immediately commit *seppuku*. It must not be lost again."

He held the head of Tomomori for a moment, looking into the eyes as if seeking the answer to a deep mystery. It was said by certain magicians that the head of one such as he now held in his graceful hand sometimes spoke immediately after death and told of things to come. He held his ear to the gaping mouth and nodded his head. All eyes were on him, both the Taira's and the Minamoto's. Raising the head above his own, he cried out, "Death has spoken to me. And the message is: Death to the Taira. Attack!"

His warriors surged forth in a rush, a raging tide of murderous, brilliant butterflies with shining steel. They advanced under a rain of shafts shot from the eager hands of the archers. Directly behind the advancing swordsmen, light lances were held in readiness. Still they neared the Taira ranks. Then seconds before the Minamoto reached the despairing Taira, they cast their lances over the heads of their own men, battering down the first rank of the enemy.

The screaming eager forces of Yeshitsune threw themselves on the Taira. Casca was passed by in the rush. He had no desire to join what was not even a battle anymore. It was slaughter.

The Taira were being beached even as their ships were being driven onto the shore. Their surviving ships were being driven to the land. Most had been cut off by the fickle currents and winds. The last he saw of Muramasa was when the little man raced past him, *Well Drinker* above his head held in both hands. The sword maker and his cursed blade thrust themselves into the hottest section of the fight.

Casca left the battlefield moving to the right flank away from the killing, closer to the beach. From there he could see all that was happening. The Taira were bunched up. The original plan of Yeshitsune to have his personal guard split the Taira in two was not applicable anymore. Since Muramasa's victory over Tomomori, the Taira were completely demoralized, even though they were ready to die.

Cavalry hit the Taira on both flanks, pushing them closer to the beach, driving them in tight where they had no room to maneuver as a rain of arrows fell on them in sheets. The pointed shafts penetrated armor and sank deep into eyes and throats. The Taira moved back again and again, closer to the edge of the water where once there they would be killed at the leisure of the victorious legions of the Minamoto.

At sea, clouds of smoke were rising to the heavens as Taira ships were burned with all on board. Those who went into the sea drowned immediately, except those few who could swim; they served as target practice for the archers on board the Minamoto ships. No prisoners. Victory or death. Gods, what a stupid way to do business! It left no options for anyone.

The *kubibukuro* were filled time and again as heads were taken by the victors. Arms, hands, even legs lay everywhere, mute evidence of the vengeance the Minamoto were taking on their enemy. They would not make the same mistakes as the Taira did and leave anyone alive who might challenge them in the future. No one would be spared.

A ship began to founder on the rocks where Casca watched the battles. It bore the pennant of the Emperor Antoku. He wondered what the eight-year-old boy was thinking at this time, when he should have been at play or learning his lessons. It was not always a good thing to be king.

Suddenly, from a cluster of black seaweed-draped boulders to his right, he saw a group of men break out and race for the beach. They were all stripped down to loincloths with their weapons slung on their backs or in their teeth. They struck out without hesitation into the water. With strong strokes they swam for the ship of the boy emperor.

That was most unusual. All of the men could swim and even more odd, none of them wore the topknot of a samurai. What were they doing? Shading his eyes to see better, he saw that the ship had struck submerged rocks and was breaking up. Most of the warriors on board were cast into the sea by the force of the tides ramming the ship onto the rocks. The rest were clinging to whatever chunk of wood or flotsam they could find. The swimmers were coming nearer to them. He didn't know who they were but something was not right. The emperor was sacred to all in this strange land. No one would kill him. It was unthinkable. At least Muramasa had told him so.

Then who were those men? And why were they even now slaughtering the few among the samurai who could swim or were clinging to bits of wreckage? He could clearly see their knives rise and fall as they finished off the *jitonari* guards of the emperor.

Straining his eyes, he saw a small gilded figure clinging to the main mast, hands clutching a line as the ship swayed and rocked beneath him. The timbers of the hull were giving way with each movement of the currents, letting more green sea into the holds, dragging the ship under.

Giving a lurch, the ship broke in half, its spine snapped by the rocks beneath. The boy Antoku was rolled into the sea. Casca saw his head surface as the youngster grasped at a line hanging over a splintered timber and hauled himself to it. Two men, samurai he knew by their topknots, were also on the heaving timber. They helped the emperor onto the timber, trying to surround him with their bodies and protect him from the sea.

Casca found himself running to the beach, casting off his clothes, armor, and weapons. Naked, he plunged into the waters and struck out for the timber that bore the son of heaven, Antoku Tenno. He didn't know what was going on, but there was no time to ask himself the question of who would order the death of Antoku and would he be interfering with someone's important plans. He didn't think, he just knew what he was doing was something that had to be done.

He didn't notice the temperature of the water as he forced his body through the surf. Striking out with strong pulls of his arms and legs, he fought the sea to reach the emperor before the swimming assassins did. He was aided in this by the samurai who surrounded Antoku. When the first two swimmers reached them, the samurai cast themselves loose from the timbers, each one grasping a swimmer in a death grip so that even if they went down under deep green waters, so would the assassins.

The *jitonari* of the imperial guard did take two of the naked swimmers with them, but the others were nearing Antoku. Casca buried his face in the saltwater and, holding his breath, stroked facedown as fast as he could to close the gap before they reached the emperor. His first contact came as a shock when one of his outreaching hands touched a wet, naked body. He didn't stop moving. Grasping the man's shoulder with his hand, he pushed him under the water, changed his grip, placed a thumb on the Adam's apple, crushed the esophagus, and moved on. The sound of the man choking to death was not heard on the surface. Casca went after the next one.

He heard a cry of alarm over the rush of the waves. Antoku was calling for help. He redoubled his efforts catching up to another of the nude swimmers. The same technique worked again. It was silent and swift. The swimmers didn't appear to have any idea that anyone would come up behind them.

Raising his head as far as he could, Casca tread water, having to wait until the waves rose up high enough so he could see the timber. Five of the swimmers were nearing the young emperor who had by now crawled to where he could straddle the timber. In his hand was a small ceremonial dagger. He held it as if he knew how to use it. The boy was prepared for what was to come. Casca could see the fear had left his face. It was as stern as that of an eight-year-old child could be. He was ready to fight and die if that was his karma.

It looked as if Antoku would die. He was too far away and the other swimmers were even now reaching out to touch the timber. Antoku's knife flashed once, then twice. Casca had the satisfaction of hearing two screams. The boy had nearly severed one man's hand at the wrist and given another a good slice across the face. Then hard callused hands grabbed the emperor and dragged him off the timber. The eager strong hands held the emperor under the water. Casca stuck out with all the force he had in his body. He reached the swimmers as the last air bubbles rose to the surface from the emperor's water-filled lungs. He grabbed one by the hair, caught him under the jaw with his other hand, and twisted. The neck snapped. Seeing him, the other swimmers pushed away from the timber, striking out for shore. Their job was done. There was no need to fight a madman in the ocean. Casca wanted to chase them but instead dove under the water and brought up the body of Antoku.

The small form was still. He had gone to his karma. Casca wished him well, for he had fought as bravely as he could and died better than many full-grown men he had known over the long years. A thin cry for help turned his head around. Not all of the swimmers had gone. One clung to a line on the timber, the man with the nearly severed hand. He begged Casca to help him. Hoisting the body of

Antoku over the timber, he grabbed the other man's wrist in a tight grip in order to stop the bleeding.

"Tell me who ordered this and I will let you live. I'll take you back to shore and turn you loose."

The man spoke, his eyes wide with fear. His face was squarer and broader than most *Nihonjin* and his accent told him what the man was. He was *ito*, a Korean, probably some noble's slave. They were the ones who handled the dead and the butchering of animals. It would have had to have been one like them to have dared to kill the emperor, but who had given the order?

Frantic, the Korean gulped seawater. He retched and spat it out with Casca's answer in the same breath.

"Yoritomo!"

Casca let his wrist go. The bright flow of arterial blood began again. The man cried out in shrill terror. "You promised you would help me!"

Casca ignored him. He had other things on his mind at the moment. Pushing the Korean off the timber, he placed himself behind it and began to paddle for shore. The Korean's last cries for help were unheard as he moved the timber with the body of Antoku lying across it to the shore.

When he broke through the surf on the beach carrying the body of Antoku, he was immediately surrounded by samurai wearing the colors of Minamoto. He was under arrest. Two of them gently took the body of the boy emperor from him. Wrapping it in costly silks, they carried it away. He saw that the

Koreans who had swam out to kill Antoku were already being lined up, kneeling on the ground, their heads extended to await the heavy slice of the *kibukiri* head-cutting swords.

Over his guards' shoulders he saw Muramasa. No one could get to him. He was surrounded by hard-faced men with the smell of recent death on them, and they wanted to use their swords again. He shook his head, indicating to Muramasa not to interfere. His hands were bound behind him and he was dragged up the beach and thrown down face first in front of Yeshitsune who sat on a soft-cushioned chair of carved teakwood.

There was something about Yeshitsune's eyes as he looked down at Casca.

"You offend me by your presence, *gaijin*. You offend me by my having to make you samurai so Muramasa-san could kill Tomomori. And now you offend me by having dared to touch the body of the Son of Heaven. Whether you were involved with these beasts," he indicated the Koreans, who were by this time totally detached from the proceedings as were their heads, "or not is of little import. Because you offend me with your ugly looks, your pale scarred body, and your bad manners, and because you offend me for touching our emperor, and because there is a remote possibility that you may have been connected with his treacherous death, I am going to punish you."

CHAPTER EIGHTEEN

Wreckage was beginning to pile up on the dark beach. Not all of the ships were in bad condition. Many could be salvaged. They had been driven on shore by their masters when they sought to escape the slaughter on the waves. It availed them naught. This had been planned for. This was the day when the stain of the Taira and all their ilk were finally put to an end and the death of Yeshitsune's and Yoritomo's father, Minamoto no Yoshimitsu, was avenged. He would send word of the victory by carrier pigeon at once to Yoritomo in Kamakura.

Also the death of Antoku Tenno would be reported. He had drowned at sea along with his mother and retainers. Very sad but very necessary. He was of Taira blood. And what did it matter whether one was eight years old or eighty? Time meant nothing, only honor. And at any age, man, woman and child were bound to honor before anything else.

Yeshitsune-sama of the Minamoto was pleased at the heads which were piled at his feet. With this he had achieved everything. His family was supreme.

The Battle of Dan-no-ura would forever be remembered with reverence among his descendants as the day of greatest glory to their name. Through him, he had guaranteed they would rule. Yoritomo Minamoto would establish the *shogunate*. He would be the first of his line to be *shogun*, military overlord of Jipongu. That was sufficient. He had served his brother and master well.

There was now nothing to be done except to take care of one small matter. The *gaijin* who had behaved with such bad manners. It was time for his judgment, and there could only be one. He would die. There was no other punishment for him, which, of course, made things so much simpler. The sword. It was all. It was everything. The beginning and the end. For at birth did not a blade sever the ties that bound one to the dark of the womb and permit him to enter the light of the sun? Without the sword there was no honor, hence no life. And with the sword came the great peace of the endless dark during which time the soul would search for rebirth. Did *gaijin*'s have souls? An interesting question but of no great import. Only the *gaijin* would find the answer to that riddle.

The heavy odor of blood washed over him. Breathing deeply, he sucked the texture of it deep into his lungs, for it was the scent of absolute power. There could never be a richer more luxurious aroma in all the world in all of time. This night he would try to find the time to write a poem to honor the occasion.

Rising gracefully from his *tatami*, he strode purposefully toward the beach, his right hand where it always was, at the hilt of his *katana*. For it to be elsewhere would be unnatural. His bodyguards surrounded him, their faces still flushed from the heat of battle. In their hands were bared blades that had only recently been wiped clean of unpure blood. Clean steel sparkled bright in the light of the day.

All fell to their faces before Yeshitsune. Only the dead of the Taira were not moved to obeisance, and this he forgave for they were no longer of import or value save in the message of their severed heads.

Muramasa watched the approach of Yeshitsune with care. He felt the power of the man in his confident stride, the feet splayed wide for better balance. The flowing of his robes all about him said this was power, final and absolute. As for the man bound at his feet, he knew there was no future for Casca-san. This was not a day in which forgiveness would be shown for even a minor offense, much less for what the barbarian had done. There was nothing for it but to bow to one's karma.

The touch of Yeshitsune's eye on him was like ice. He knew he had been singled out. At the proper distance he knelt, lowering his head to the earth before the master of the land of the gods. He waited. This day one never knew what would come next, the command to slit one's belly or a reward.

"Muramasa-san. Rise. I have seen your work this day."

As Muramasa rose he felt a slight pressure on his shoulders. Yesitsune had taken off his own bloodstained cloak and laid it upon his shoulders. About him he could hear the hissing of awe and wonder at the honor being given him. He was most favored.

Carefully he raised his eyes to the stern tight-lipped face of the master. "Ah, Yeshitsune-sama. It is too much, this honor. I have done nothing to warrant such honor."

He bowed lower, hissing between his teeth.

"Muramasa-san. I have seen few in my life with such sword work as you have shown this day. I knew that the *shini-mono-gurui*, the hour of the death fury, was upon you. I saw your blade drink many times. Is it true that the *katana* which you so aptly named *Well Drinker* was made by yourself?"

Again the gasps of awe at the recognition their master was showing this *ronin*.

"Yes, Lord. It is so."

"May I see the blade, Muramasa-san."

In spite of himself he felt the pride well up in his breast. And his face flushed as he fought to control his emotions. To show such would demean the moment.

Dropping to both knees in the formal kneeling position, he withdrew *Well Drinker*, leaving it in its scabbard. With head bowed, arms extended, he offered it to Yeshitsune.

Taking the *katana* in its engraved sharkskin scabbard, he pulled the blade out a few inches and sucked at his teeth in appreciation of the workmanship. "May I take *Well Drinker* out of its shelter, Muramasa-san?"

"I would be honored, Lord." Muramasa bowed deeper. Carefully, with extreme grace, Yeshitsune bared the blade. With the eye of a master, he examined the detail of the work, the delicate watering of the patterns of the blade. The sword was alive in his hand. It was indeed one that would have to drink from the well of life and drink often. It moved with a life of its own, a life that transmitted itself up his arm with a shiver. It lived and was more than anything he'd ever experienced. He would almost trade this day to possess such an article of beauty and life.

Catching a look at the face of the master as he dared to raise his eyes a fraction, Muramasa saw the expression on the *daimyo*'s face as he held *Well Drinker* in his hand. He knew what was happening, for had it not been the same for him? The blade was claiming another. In life as in death, the *Well Drinker* could not be denied.

Hardly daring to speak, he hissed between his teeth, "Lord. If I may speak?"

Absently, Yeshitsune nodded his head. "Of course."

"There are few times in one's life during which a thing or a life is absolutely made for another. I feel that *Well Drinker* no longer calls to me, that he has found a new master. Am I not correct in this matter, Lord?"

Raising the blade over his head to catch the light, he moved it in one swift graceful arc. He made the *jumonji*, the crosswise cut.

The Korean slave blinked, opened his mouth to cry out, but nothing came forth as the upper half of his body separated from the left shoulder to the right hip. It slid slowly apart. *Well Drinker* had gone to the fountain again.

The escape of held breath was heard all around. Heads bobbed in admiration at the cleanness of the stroke, the gentleness of the cut that slid through the man's bones and flesh as if through the belly of a fat woman. *Well Drinker* most assuredly was a work of art.

Yeshitsune removed a scarlet silk scarf from his sleeve and cleansed the blade with care before returning it to its scabbard. Never had the feel of a cut been so sensuous, so . . . so right. This blade was made for him. Never would it leave his side.

"Muramasa-san. *Domo, genki desu.* I accept your gift. Knowing that I have nothing to offer you that could be its equal, I am therefore eternally in your debt. I would like, however, to let all present know that from this day forth I shall request of my brother that you shall be *Hogen.*"

Muramasa felt his legs tremble. He feared he would lose consciousness. He had been given the highest of the three honors that could be conferred upon an artist.

Yeshitsune felt expansive. Yet not to reward such a gift greatly was to demean the gift. *Well Drinker* would not be shamed. He continued, "In addition I make you *To-zama.*" It was the third rank of nobility. He was now samurai.

"We shall discuss your fife and the amount of

koku you will need later. Now is there any other
wish that I may grant you this day?''

Yeshitsune's hand helped him to his feet. Muramasa
kept his eyes lowered to avoid Yeshitsune's being
able to read anything in them.

"Yes, Lord. Now that you have honored me with
glory and gifts of which I am not deserving, I must
as always serve you the best I can. Let me judge the
barbarian's punishment, for he has by his actions
betrayed me as well.''

"You wish to take his head Muramasa-san?''

"*Aiie,* no, Lord. He is a foreign animal. I would
not wish to stain the sword of a samurai with his
unclean blood. It was I who who found him on the
beach washed up by a storm. The sea brought him to
this land. Let it take him back. Let us tie him to a
timber and set him upon the tide. There the sun, salt,
and beasts of the dark waters may claim him. His
death might take days, for he is very strong. And he
will have plenty of time to reflect upon his lack of
manners. Let the seas and the birds have him. He is
not worthy of a quick death.''

Yeshitsune almost smiled. That was good. This
new samurai sword maker of his had imagination
and it was poetic in its way. It was fitting that the
barbarian should be sent away in the manner he had
been brought to them. That he could survive such a
punishment was so remote a possibility as to be
impossible to calculate. However, if by some mira-
cle he did live, then that, too, was his karma to do
so.

"As you say, Muramasa-san. It is fitting. The beast is yours. Take him."

Muramasa bowed, torn by his feelings. Casca-san had been a good companion to him. He had fought well and never failed him—until now. Or had he? What he had done was most strange. Not that he believed for an instant that Casca had planned on killing or was even involved with the killing of Antoku. No! He had gotten in the way of Yeshitsune who had never liked him and who was using this as an excuse to get rid of him.

He, too, had witnessed the rapid executions of the Koreans before they had a chance to talk to anyone. He did not like what had to be done but he was certain of two things. Casca-san did not belong in these islands. The other was that he had the feeling Casca-san would survive. The scar-faced, gray-eyed man would not die, though his suffering would be terrible.

The guards kept Casca's hands bound as they led him back to the beach where Muramasa supervised the tying of his body to a broken beam, the same one he had brought Antoku to shore with.

During all this, Casca said nothing, only watched the eyes of his sword mate.

The beam would be taken in tow by one of Yoritomo's ships and hauled out to the open seas beyond the straits where it would be cast loose upon the waves. Casca was aware of this and still he said nothing.

Muramasa pushed the mast out beyond the surf

by himself as he entered the water to where his chest
was reached by the foam. His hands made rapid
moves beneath the waves. The ropes binding Casca
were nearly severed by a stroke of his knife. With
Casca's great strength he would have no trouble in
setting himself free.

As the towing ship took up the slack and hauled
the beam out, Muramasa said in a voice that none
but Casca could hear, "Go away from us and do not
come back. There are enough curses in this land.
Today I am free of two. Go away, my friend."

The waves lapped over him as the distance grew
between him and Muramasa. The last thing Casca
heard as he drifted over the rush of the waves was:

"Take this with you, Casca-san, wherever you
go. You are now and will always be SAMURAI!"

THE ETERNAL MERCENARY
By Barry Sadler